M.E Braddon

Vixen
Volume 2

M.E Braddon

Vixen
Volume 2

1st Edition | ISBN: 978-3-75237-382-0

Place of Publication: Frankfurt am Main, Germany

Year of Publication: 2020

Outlook Verlag GmbH, Germany.

Reproduction of the original.

VIXEN

BY
M. E. BRADDON

VOL. II.

CHAPTER I.

"Shall I tell you the Secret?"

For the rest of the way Violet walked with Mrs. Scobel, and at the garden-gate of the Vicarage Roderick Vawdrey wished them both good-night, and tramped off, with his basket on his back and his rod on his shoulder, for the long walk to Briarwood.

Here the children separated, and ran off to their scattered homes, dropping grateful bob-curtsies to the last—"louting," as they called it in their Forest dialect.

"You must come in and have some tea, Violet," said Mrs. Scobel. "You must be very tired."

"I am rather tired; but I think it's too late for tea. I had better get home at once."

"Ignatius shall see you home, my dear," cried Mrs. Scobel. At which the indefatigable Vicar, who had shouted himself hoarse in leading his choir, protested himself delighted to escort Miss Tempest.

The church clock struck ten as they went along the narrow forest-path between Beechdale and the Abbey House.

"Oh," cried Vixen, "I do hope mamma's people will have gone home."

A carriage rolled past them as they came out into the road.

"That's Mrs. Carteret's landau," said Vixen. "I breathe more freely. And there goes Mrs. Horwood's brougham; so I suppose everything is over. How nice it is when one's friends are so unanimous in their leave-taking."

"I shall try to remember that the next time I dine at the Abbey House," said Mr. Scobel laughing.

"Oh, please don't!" cried Violet. "You and Mrs. Scobel are different. I don't mind you; but those dreadful stiff old ladies mamma cultivates, who think of nothing but their dress and their own importance—a little of them goes a very long way."

"But, my dear Miss Tempest, the Carterets and the Horwoods are some of the best people in the neighbourhood."

"Of course they are," answered Vixen. "If they were not they would hardly venture to be so stupid. They take the full license of their acres and their quarterings. People with a coat-of-arms found yesterday, and no land to speak of, are obliged to make themselves agreeable."

2

"Like Captain Winstanley," suggested Mr. Scobel. "I don't suppose he has land enough to sod a lark. But he is excellent company."

"Very," assented Vixen, "for the people who like him."

They were at the gate by this time.

"You shan't come any further unless you are coming in to see mamma," protested Vixen.

"Thanks, no; it's too late to think of that."

"Then go home immediately, and have some supper," said Vixen imperatively. "You've had nothing but a cup of weak tea since two o'clock this afternoon. You must be worn out."

"On such an occasion as to-day a man must not think of himself," said the Vicar.

"I wonder when you ever do think of yourself," said Vixen.

And indeed Mr. Scobel, like many another Anglican pastor of modern times, led a life which, save for its liberty to go where he listed, and to talk as much as he liked, was but little less severe in its exactions upon the flesh and the spirit than that of the monks of La Trappe.

The Abbey House looked very quiet when Vixen went into the hall, whose doors stood open to the soft spring night. The servants were all at supper, treating themselves to some extra comforts on the strength of a dinner-party, and talking over the evening's entertainment and its bearings on their mistress's life. There was a feeling in the servants' hall that these little dinners, however seeming harmless, had a certain bent and tendency inimical to the household, and household peace.

"He was more particular in his manner to-night than hever," said the butler, as he dismembered a duck which had been "hotted up" after removal from the dining-room. "He feels hisself master of the whole lot of us already. I could see it in his hi. 'Is that the cabinet 'ock, Forbes?' he says to me, when I was a-filling round after the bait. 'No,' says I, 'it is not. We ain't got so much of our cabinet 'ocks that we can afford to trifle with 'em.' Of course I said it in a hundertone, confidential like; but I wanted him to know who was master of the cellar."

"There'll be nobody master but him when once he gets his foot inside these doors," said Mrs. Trimmer, the housekeeper, with a mournful shake of her head. "No, Porline, I'll have a noo pertater. Them canister peas ain't got no flaviour with them."

While they were enjoying themselves, with a certain chastening touch of prophetic melancholy, in the servants' hall, Violet was going slowly upstairs and along the corridor which led past her mother's rooms.

"I must go in and wish mamma good-night," she thought; "though I am pretty sure of a lecture for my pains."

Just at this moment a door opened, and a soft voice called "Violet," pleadingly.

"Dear mamma, I was just coming in to say good-night."

"Were you, darling? I heard your footstep, and I was afraid you were going by. And I want very particularly to see you to-night, Violet."

"Do you, mamma? I hope not to scold me for going with the school-children. They had such a happy afternoon; and ate! it was like a miracle. Not so little serving for so many, but so few devouring so much."

Pamela Tempest put her arm round her daughter, and kissed her, with more warmth of affection than she had shown since the sad days after the Squire's death. Violet looked at her mother wonderingly. She could hardly see the widow's fair delicate face in the dimly-lighted room. It was one of the prettiest rooms in the house—half boudoir half dressing-room, crowded with elegant luxuries and modern inventions, gipsy tables, book-stands, toy-cabinets of egg-shell china, a toilet table *à la* Pompadour, a writing-desk *à la* Sevigné. Such small things had made the small joys of Mrs. Tempest's life. When she mourned her kind husband, she lamented him as the someone who had bought her everything she wanted.

She had taken off her dinner-dress, and looked particularly fair and youthful in her soft muslin dressing-gown, trimmed with Mechlin lace which had cost as much as a small holding on the outskirts of the Forest. Even in that subdued light Violet could see that her mother's cheeks were pinker than usual, that her eyes were clouded with tears, and her manner anxiously agitated.

"Mamma," cried the girl, "there is something wrong, I know. Something has happened."

"There is nothing wrong, love. But something has happened. Something which I hope will not make you unhappy—for it has made me very happy."

"You are talking in enigmas, mamma, and I am too tired to be good at guessing riddles, just now," said Violet, becoming suddenly cold as ice.

A few moments ago she had been all gentleness and love, responding to the unwonted affection of her mother's caresses. Now she drew herself away and stood aloof, with her heart beating fast and furiously. She divined what was coming. She had guessed the riddle already.

4

"Come and sit by the fire, Violet, and I will tell you—everything," said Mrs. Tempest coaxingly, seating herself in the low semi-circular chair which was her especial delight.

"I can hear what you have to tell just as well where I am," answered Violet curtly, walking to the latticed window, which was open to the night. The moon was shining over the rise and fall of the woods; the scent of the flowers came stealing up from the garden. Without, all was calm and sweetness, within, fever and smothered wrath. "I can't think how you can endure a fire on such a night. The room is positively stifling."

"Ah Violet, you have not my sad susceptibility to cold."

"No, mamma. I don't keep myself shut up like an unset diamond in a jeweller's strong-box."

"I don't think I can tell you—the little secret I have to tell, Violet, unless you come over to me and sit by my side, and give me your hand, and let me feel as if you were really fond of me," pleaded Mrs. Tempest, with a little gush of piteousness. "You seem like an enemy, standing over there with your back to me, looking out at the sky."

"Perhaps there is no need for you to tell me anything, mamma," answered Violet, in a tone which, to that tremulous listener in the low seat by the fire, sounded as severe as the voice of a judge pronouncing sentence. "Shall I tell you the secret?"

There was no answer.

"Shall I, mamma?"

"I don't think you can, my love."

"Yes, I am afraid I can. The secret—which is no secret to me or to anyone else in the world, any more than the place where the ostrich has put his head is a secret when his body is sticking up out of the sand—the secret is that, after being for seventeen happy honourable years the wife of the best and truest of men—the kindest, most devoted, and most generous of husbands—you are going to take another husband, who comes to you with no better credentials than a smooth tongue and a carefully-drilled figure, and who will punish your want of faith and constancy to my dead father by making the rest of your life miserable—as you will deserve that it shall be. Yes, mother, I, your only child, say so. You will deserve to be wretched if you marry Captain Winstanley."

The widow gave a faint scream, half indignation, half terror. For the moment she felt as if some prophetic curse had been hurled upon her. The tall straight figure in the white gown, standing in the full flood of moonlight,

5

looked awful as Cassandra, prophesying death and doom in the wicked house at Argos.

"It is too bad," sobbed Mrs. Tempest; "it is cruel, undutiful, disrespectful, positively wicked for a daughter to talk to a mother as you have talked to me to-night. How can Miss McCroke have brought you up, I wonder, that you are capable of using such language? Have you forgotten the Fifth Commandment?"

"No. It tells me to honour my father and my mother. I honour my dead father, I honour you, when I try to save you from the perdition of a second marriage."

"Perdition!" echoed Mrs. Tempest faintly, "what language!"

"I knew when that adventurer came here, that he intended to make himself master of this house—to steal my dead father's place," cried Vixen passionately.

"You have no right to call him an adventurer. He is an officer and a gentleman. You offer him a cruel, an unprovoked insult. You insult me still more deeply by your abuse of him. Am I so old, or so ugly, or so altogether horrid, that a man cannot love me for my own sake?"

"Not such a man as Captain Winstanley. He does not know what love means. He would have made me marry him if he could, because I am to have the estate by-and-bye. Failing that, he has made you accept him for your husband. Yes, he has conquered you, as a cat conquers a bird, fascinating the poor wretch with its hateful green eyes. You are quite young enough and pretty enough to win a good man's regard, if you were a penniless unprotected widow, needing a husband to shelter you and provide for you. But you are the natural victim of such a man as Captain Winstanley."

"You are altogether unjust and unreasonable," exclaimed Mrs. Tempest, weeping copiously. "Your poor dear father spoiled you. No one but a spoiled child would talk as you are talking. Who made you a judge of Captain Winstanley? It is not true that he ever wanted to marry you. I don't believe it for an instant."

"Very well, mother. If you are wilfully blind——"

"I am not blind. I have lived twice as long as you have. I am a better judge of human nature than you can be."

"Not of your admirer's, your flatterer's nature," cried Vixen. "He has slavered you with pretty speeches and soft words, as the cobra slavers his victim, and he will devour you, as the cobra does. He will swallow up your peace of mind, your self-respect, your independence, your money—all good

6

things you possess. He will make you contemptible in the eyes of all who know you. He will make you base in your own eyes."

"It is not true. You are blinded by prejudice."

"I want to save you from yourself, if I can."

"You are too late to save me, as you call it. Captain Winstanley has touched my heart by his patient devotion, I have not been so easily won as you seem to imagine. I have refused him three times. He knows that I had made up my mind never to marry again. Nothing was farther from my thoughts than a second marriage. I liked him as a companion and friend. That he knew. But I never intended that he should be more to me than a friend. He knew that. His patience has conquered me. Such devotion as he has given me has not often been offered to a woman. I do not think any woman living could resist it. He is all that is good and noble, and I am assured, Violet, that as a second father——"

Vixen interrupted her with a cry of horror.

"For God's sake, mamma, do not utter the word 'father' in conjunction with his name. He may become your husband—I have no power to prevent that evil—but he shall never call himself my father."

"What happiness can there be for any of us, Violet, when you start with such prejudices?" whimpered Mrs. Tempest.

"I do not expect there will be much," said Vixen. "Good-night, mamma."

"You are very unkind. You won't even stop to hear how it came about—how Conrad persuaded me to forego my determination."

"No, mamma. I don't want to hear the details. The fact is enough for me. If it would be any use for me to go down upon my knees and entreat you to give up this man, I would gladly do it; but I fear it would be no use."

"It would not. Violet," answered the widow, with modest resoluteness. "I have given Conrad my word. I cannot withdraw it."

"Then I have nothing more to say," replied Vixen, with her hand upon the door, "except good-night."

"You will not even kiss me?"

"Excuse me, mamma; I am not in a kissing humour."

And so Vixen left her.

Mrs. Tempest sat by the fading fire, and cried herself into a gentle slumber. It was very hard. She had longed to pour the story of this second courtship—

its thrilling, unexpected joys, its wondrous surprises—into a sympathetic ear. And Violet, the natural recipient of these gentle confidences, had treated her so cruelly.

She felt herself sorely ill-used; and then came soothing thoughts about her *trousseau*, her wedding-dress, the dress in which she should start for her wedding-tour. All things would of course be chastened and subdued. No woman can be a bride twice in her life; but Mrs. Tempest meant that the *trousseau* should, in its way, be perfect. There should be no rush or excitement in the preparation; nothing should be scamped or hurried. Calmness, deliberation, and a faultless taste should pervade all things.

"I will have no trimming but Valenciennes for my under-linen," she decided; "it is the only lace that never offends. And I will have old English monograms in satin-stitch upon everything. My *peignoirs* will require a good deal of study; they admit of so much variety. I will have only a few dresses, but those shall be from Paris. Theodore must go over and get them from Worth. She knows what suits me better than I do myself. I am not going to be extravagant, but Conrad so appreciates elegance and taste; and of course he will wish me to be well dressed."

And so, comforted by these reflections, Mrs. Tempest sank into a gentle slumber, from which she was awakened by Pauline, who had discussed her mistress's foolishness over a hearty supper, and now came to perform the duties of the evening toilet.

"Oh Pauline," cried the widow, with a shiver, "I'm glad you awoke me. I've just had such an awful dream."

"Lor', ma'am! What about?"

"Oh, an awful dream. I thought Madame Theodore sent me home a *trousseau* and that there was not a single thing that would fit. I looked an object in every one of the dresses."

CHAPTER II.

Wedding Garments.

After that night Vixen held her peace. There were no more bitter words between Mrs. Tempest and her daughter, but the mother knew that there was a wellspring of bitterness—a Marah whose waters were inexhaustible—in her daughter's heart; and that domestic happiness, under one roof, was henceforth impossible for these two.

There were very few words of any kind between Violet and Mrs Tempest at this time. The girl kept herself as much as possible apart from her mother. The widow lived her languid drawing-room life, dawdling away long slow days that left no more impression behind them than the drift of rose-leaves across the velvet lawn before her windows. A little point-lace, deftly worked by slim white fingers flashing with gems; a little Tennyson; a little Owen Meredith; a little Browning—only half understood at best; a little scandal; a great deal of orange pekoe, sipped out of old Worcester teacups of royal blue or flowered Swansea; an hour's letter-writing on the last fashionable note-paper; elegantly-worded inanity, delicately penned in a flowing Italian hand, with long loops to the Y's and G's, and a serpentine curve at the end of every word.

No life could well have been more useless or vapid. Even Mrs. Tempest's charities—those doles of wine and soup, bread and clothing, which are looked for naturally from the mistress of a fine old mansion—were vicarious. Trimmer, the housekeeper, did everything. Indeed, in the eyes of the surrounding poor, Mrs. Trimmer was mistress of the Abbey House. It was to her they looked for relief; it was her reproof they feared; and to her they louted lowest. The faded beauty, reclining in her barouche, wrapped in white raiment of softest China crape, and whirling past them in a cloud of dust, was as remote as a goddess. They could hardly have realised that she was fashioned out of the same clay that made themselves.

Upon so smooth and eventless an existence Captain Winstanley's presence came like a gust of north wind across the sultry languor of an August noontide. His energy, his prompt, resolute manner of thinking and acting upon all occasions, impressed Mrs. Tempest with an extraordinary sense of his strength of mind and manliness. It seemed to her that she must always be safe where he was. No danger, no difficulty could assail her while his strong arm was there to ward it off. She felt very much as Mary Stuart may have done about Bothwell; when, moved to scornful aversion by the silken boy-profligate Darnley, her heart acknowledged its master in the dark freebooter who had slain him. There had been no Darnley in Pamela Tempest's life; but this resolute, clear-brained soldier was her Bothwell. She had the Mary Stuart temperament, the love of compliments and fine dresses, dainty needlework and luxurious living, without the Stuart craft. In Conrad Winstanley she had found her master, and she was content to be so mastered; willing to lay down her little sum of power at his feet, and live henceforward like a tame falcon at the end of a string. Her position, as a widow, was an excellent one. The Squire's will had been dictated in fullest confidence in his wife's goodness and discretion; and doubtless also with the soothing idea common to most hale and healthy men, that it must be a long time before their testamentary arrangements can come into effect. It was a holograph will, and the Squire's own composition throughout. "He would have no lawyer's finger in that pie," he had said. The disposal of his estate had cost him many hours of painful thought before he rang the bell for his bailiff and his butler, and executed it in their presence.

Mrs. Tempest was mistress of the Abbey House for her life; and at her death it was to become Violet's property. Violet was not to come of age until she was twenty-five, and in the meantime her mother was to be her sole guardian, and absolute mistress of everything. There was no question of an allowance for the maintenance of the heiress, no question as to the accumulation of income. Everything was to belong to Mrs. Tempest till Violet came of age. She had only to educate and maintain her daughter in whatever manner she might think fit. At Violet's majority the estate was to pass into her possession, charged with an income of fifteen hundred a year, to be paid to the widow for her lifetime. Until her twenty-fifth birthday, therefore, Violet was in the position of a child, entirely dependent on her mother's liberality, and bound to obey her mother as her natural and only guardian. There was no court of appeal nearer than the Court of Chancery. There was no one to whom the two women could make their complaints or refer their differences.

Naturally, Captain Winstanley had long before this made himself acquainted with the particulars of the Squire's will. For six years he saw himself sole master of a very fine estate, and at the end of six years reduced to an income which seemed, comparatively, a pittance, and altogether inadequate for the maintenance of such a place as the Abbey House. Still, fifteen hundred a year and the Abbey House were a long way on the right side of nothing: and Captain Winstanley felt that he had fallen on his feet.

That was a dreary June for Vixen. She hugged her sorrow, and lived in a mental solitude which was almost awful in so young a soul. She made a confidante of no one, not even of kind-hearted Mrs. Scobel, who was quite ready to pity her and condole with her, and who was secretly indignant at the widow's folly.

The fact of Mrs. Tempest's intended marriage had become known to all her friends and neighbours, with the usual effect of such intelligence. Society said sweet things to her; and praised Captain Winstanley; and hoped the wedding would be soon; and opined that it would be quite a nice thing for Miss Tempest to have such an agreeable stepfather, with whom she could ride to hounds as she had done with the dear Squire. And the same society, driving away from the Abbey House in its landaus and pony-carriages, after half-an-hour's pleasant gossip and a cup of delicately flavoured tea, called Mrs. Tempest a fool, and her intended husband an adventurer.

Vixen kept aloof from all the gossip and tea-drinking. She did not even go near her old friends the Scobels, in these days of smothered wrath and slow consuming indignation. She deserted the schools, her old pensioners, even the little village children, to whom she had loved to carry baskets of good things, and pocketfuls of halfpence, and whose queer country dialect had seemed as sweet to her as the carolling of finches and blackbirds in the woods. Everything in the way of charity was left to Mrs. Trimmer now. Vixen took her long solitary rides in the Forest, roaming wherever there was a footway for her horse under the darkening beeches, dangerously near the swampy ground where the wet grass shone in the sunlight, the green reedy patches that meant peril; into the calm unfathomable depths of Mark Ash, or Queen's Bower; up to the wild heathy crest of Boldrewood; wherever there was loneliness and beauty.

Roderick had gone to London for the season, and was riding with Lady Mabel in the Row, or dancing attendance at garden-parties, exhibitions, and flower-shows.

"I wonder how he likes the dusty days, and the crowded rooms, the classical music, and high-art exhibitions?" thought Vixen savagely. "I wonder how he likes being led about like a Pomeranian terrier? I don't think I could endure it if I were a man. But I suppose when one is in love——"

And then Vixen thought of their last talk together, and how little of the lover's enthusiasm there was in Roderick's mention of his cousin.

"In the bottom of my heart I know that he is going to marry her for the sake of her estate, or because his mother wished it and urged it, and he was too weak-minded to go on saying No. I would not say it for the world, or let anyone else say it in my hearing, but, in my heart of hearts, I know he does not love her."

And then, after a thoughtful silence, she cried to the mute unresponsive woods:

"Oh, it is wicked, abominable, mad, to marry without love!"

The woods spoke to her of Roderick Vawdrey. How often she had ridden by his side beneath these spreading beech-boughs, dipping her childish head, just as she dipped it to-day, under the low branches, steering her pony carefully between the prickly holly-bushes, plunging deep into the hollows where the dry leaves crackled under his hoofs.

"I fancied Rorie and I were to spend our lives together—somehow," she said to herself. "It seems very strange for us to be quite parted."

She saw Mr. Vawdrey's name in the fashionable newspapers, in the lists of guests at dinners and drums. London life suited him very well, no doubt. She heard that he was a member of the Four-in-hand Club, and turned out in splendid style at Hyde Park Corner. There was no talk yet of his going into Parliament. That was an affair of the future.

Since that evening on which Mrs. Tempest announced her intention of taking a second husband, Violet and Captain Winstanley had only met in the presence of other people. The Captain had tried to infuse a certain fatherly familiarity into his manner; but Vixen had met every attempt at friendliness with a sullen disdain, which kept even Captain Winstanley at arm's length.

"We shall understand each other better by-and-by," he said to himself, galled by this coldness. "It would be a pity to disturb these halcyon days by anything in the way of a scene. I shall know how to manage Miss Tempest—afterwards."

He spoke of her, and to her, always as Miss Tempest. He had never called her Violet since that night in the Pavilion garden.

These days before her wedding were indeed a halcyon season for Mrs. Tempest. She existed in an atmosphere of millinery and pretty speeches. Her attention was called away from a ribbon by the sweet distraction of a compliment, and oscillated between tender whispers and honiton lace. Conrad Winstanley was a delightful lover. His enemies would have said that he had done the same kind of thing so often, that it would have been strange if he had not done it well. His was assuredly no 'prentice hand in the art. Poor Mrs. Tempest lived in a state of mild intoxication, as dreamily delicious as the effects of opium. She was enchanted with her lover, and still better pleased with herself. At nine-and-thirty it was very sweet to find herself exercising so potent an influence over the Captain's strong nature. She could not help comparing herself to Cleopatra, and her lover to Antony. If he had not thrown away a world for her sake, he was at least ready to abandon the busy career which a man loves, and to devote his future existence to rural domesticity. He confessed that he had been hardened by much contact with the world, that he did not love now for the first time; but he told his betrothed that her influence had awakened feelings which had never before been called into life, that this love which he felt for her was to all intents and purposes a first love, the first pure and perfect affection that had subjugated and elevated his soul.

After that night in Mrs. Tempest's boudoir, it was only by tacit avoidance of her mother that Vixen showed the intensity of her disapproval. If she could have done any good by reproof or entreaty, by pleading or exhortation, she would assuredly have spoken; but she saw the Captain and her mother together every day, and she knew that, opposed to his influence, her words were like the idle wind which bloweth where it listeth. So she held her peace, and looked on with an aching angry heart, and hated the intruder who had come to steal her dead father's place. To take her father's place; that in Violet's mind was the unpardonable wrong. That any man should enter that house as master, and sit in the Squire's seat, and rule the Squire's servants, and ride the Squire's horses, was an outrage beyond endurance. She might have looked more leniently on her mother's folly, had the widow chosen a second husband with a house and home of his own, who would have carried off his wife to reign over his own belongings, and left the Abbey House desolate—a temple dedicated to the dead.

Mrs. Tempest's manner towards her daughter during this period was at once conciliatory and reproachful. She felt it a hard thing that Violet should have taken up such an obnoxious position. This complaint she repeated piteously, with many variations, when she discussed Violet's unkindness with her lover. She had no secrets from the Captain, and she told him all the bitter things Violet had said about him.

He heard her with firmly-set lips and an angry sparkle in his dark eyes, but his tone was full of paternal indulgence presently, when Mrs. Tempest had poured out all her woes.

"Is it not hard upon me, Conrad?" she asked in conclusion.

"My dear Pamela, I hope you are too strong-minded to distress yourself seriously about a wilful girl's foolishness. Your daughter has a noble nature, but she has been spoiled by too much indulgence. Even a race-horse—the noblest thing in creation—has to be broken in; not always without severe punishment. Miss Tempest and I will come to understand each other perfectly by-and-by."

"I know you will be a second father to her," said Mrs. Tempest tearfully.

"I will do my duty to her, dearest, be assured."

Still Mrs. Tempest went on harping upon the cruelty of her daughter's conduct. The consciousness of Violet's displeasure weighed heavily upon her.

"I dare not even show her my *trousseau*," she complained, "all confidence is at an end between us. I should like to have had her opinion about my dresses—though she is sadly deficient in taste, poor child! and has never even learnt to put on her gloves perfectly."

"And your own taste is faultless, love," replied the Captain soothingly. "What can you want with advice from an inexperienced girl, whose mind is in the stable?"

"It is not her advice I want, Conrad; but her sympathy. Fanny Scobel is coming this afternoon. I can show her my things. I really feel quite nervous about talking to Violet of her own dress. She must have a new dress for the wedding, you know; though she cannot be a bridesmaid. I think that is really unfair. Don't you, Conrad?"

"What is unfair, dearest?" asked the Captain, whose mind had scarcely followed the harmless meanderings of his lady's speech.

"That a widow is not allowed to have bridesmaids or orange-blossoms. It seems like taking the poetry out of a wedding, does it not?"

"Not to my mind, Pamela. The poetry of wedlock does not lie in these details—a sugared cake, and satin favours; a string of carriages, and a Brussels veil. The true poetry of marriage is in the devotion and fidelity of the two hearts it binds together."

Mrs Tempest sighed gently, and was almost resigned to be married without bridesmaids or orange-blossoms.

It was now within a month of the wedding, which was to be solemnised on the last day of August—a convenient season for a honeymoon tour in Scotland. Mrs. Tempest liked to travel when other people travelled. Mountain and flood would have had scarcely any charm for her "out of the season." The time had come when Violet's dress must be talked about, as Mrs. Tempest told the Vicar's wife solemnly. She had confided the secret of her daughter's unkindness to Mrs. Scobel, in the friendly hour of afternoon tea.

"It is very hard upon me," she repeated—"very hard that the only drawback to my happiness should come from my own child."

"Violet was so fond of her father," said Mrs. Scobel excusingly.

"But is that any reason she should treat me unkindly? Who could have been fonder of dear Edward than I was? I studied his happiness in everything. There never was an unkind word between us. I do not think anyone could expect me to go down to my grave a widow, in order to prove my affection for my dearest Edward. That was proved by every act of my married life. I have nothing to regret, nothing to atone for. I feel myself free to reward Captain Winstanley's devotion. He has followed me from place to place for the last two years; and has remained constant, in spite of every rebuff. He proposed to me three times before I accepted him."

Mrs. Scobel had been favoured with the history of these three separate offers more than once.

"I know, dear Mrs. Tempest," she said somewhat hurriedly, lest her friend should recapitulate the details. "He certainly seems very devoted. But, of course, from a worldly point of view, you are an excellent match for him."

"Do you think I would marry him if I thought that consideration had any weight with him?" demanded Mrs. Tempest indignantly. And Mrs. Scobel could say no more.

There are cases of physical blindness past the skill of surgery, but there is no blindness more incurable than that of a woman on the verge of forty who fancies herself beloved.

"But Violet's dress for the wedding," said Mrs. Scobel, anxious to get the conversation upon safer ground. "Have you really said nothing to her about it?"

"No. She is so headstrong and self-willed. I have been absolutely afraid to speak. But it must be settled immediately. Theodore is always so busy. It will be quite a favour to get the dress made at so short a notice, I daresay."

"Why not speak to Violet this afternoon?"

"While you are here? Yes, I might do that," replied Mrs. Tempest eagerly.

She felt she could approach the subject more comfortably in Mrs. Scobel's presence. There would be a kind of protection in a third person. She rang the bell.

"Has Miss Tempest come home from her ride?"

"Yes, ma'am. She has just come in."

"Send her to me at once then. Ask her not to stop to change her dress."

Mrs. Tempest and Mrs. Scobel were in the drawing-room, sitting at a gipsy table before an open window; the widow wrapped in a China-crape shawl, lest even the summer breeze should be too chill for her delicate frame, the Worcester cups and saucers, and antique silver tea pot and caddy and kettle set out before her, like a child's toys.

Violet came running in, flushed after her ride, her habit muddy.

"Bogged again!" cried Mrs. Tempest, with ineffable disgust. "That horse will be the death of you some day."

"I think not, mamma. How do you do, Mrs. Scobel?"

"Violet," said the Vicar's wife gravely, "why do you never come to our

15

week-day services now?"

"I—I—don't know. I have not felt in the humour for coming to church. It's no use to come and kneel in a holy place with rebellious thoughts in my heart. I come on Sundays for decency's sake; but I think it is better to keep away from the week-day services till I am in a better temper."

"I don't think that's quite the way to recover your temper, dear."

Violet was silent, and there was a rather awkward pause.

"Will you have a cup of tea, dear?" asked Mrs. Tempest.

"No, thanks, mamma. I think, unless you have something very particular to say to me, I had better take my muddy habit off your carpet. I feel rather warm and dusty. I shall be glad to change my dress."

"But I have something very particular to say, Violet. I won't detain you long. You'd better have a cup of tea."

"Just as you please, mamma."

And forgetful of her clay-bespattered habit, Violet sank into one of the satin-covered chairs, and made a wreck of an antimacassar worked in crewels by Mrs. Tempest's own hands.

"I am going to write to Madame Theodore by this evening's post, Violet," said her mother, handing her a cup of tea, and making believe not to see the destruction of that exquisite antimacassar; "and I should like to order your dress—for—the wedding. I have been thinking that cream-colour and pale blue would suit you to perfection. A cream-coloured hat—the Vandyck shape —with a long blue ostrich——"

"Please don't take any trouble about it, mamma," said Vixen, whose cheek had paled at the word "wedding," and who now sat very erect in her chair, holding her cup and saucer firmly. "I am not going to be present at your wedding, so I shall not want a dress."

"Violet!" cried Mrs. Tempest, beginning to tremble. "You cannot mean what you say. You have been very unkind, very undutiful. You have made me perfectly miserable for the last seven weeks; but I cannot believe that you would—grossly insult me—by refusing to be present at my wedding."

"I do not wish to insult you, mamma. I am very sorry if I have pained you; but I cannot and will not be present at a marriage the very idea of which is hateful to me. If my presence could give any sanction to this madness of yours, that sanction shall not be given."

"Violet, have you thought what you are doing? Have you considered what will be said—by the world?"

"I think the world—our world—must have made up its mind about your second marriage already, mamma," Vixen answered quietly. "My absence from your wedding can make very little difference."

"It will make a very great difference; and you know it!" cried Mrs. Tempest, roused to as much passion as she was capable of feeling. "People will say that my daughter sets her face against my marriage—my daughter, who ought to sympathise with me, and rejoice that I have found a true friend and protector."

"I cannot either sympathise or rejoice, mamma. It is much better that I should stop away from your wedding. I should look miserable, and make other people uncomfortable."

"Your absence will humiliate and lower me in the sight of my friends. It will be a disgrace. And yet you take this course on purpose to wound and injure me. You are a wicked undutiful daughter."

"Oh, mamma!" cried Vixen, with grave voice and reproachful eyes—eyes before whose steady gaze the tearful widow drooped and trembled, "is duty so one-sided? Do I owe all to you, and you nothing to me? My father left us together, mother and daughter, to be all the world to each other. He left us mistresses of the dear old home we had shared with him. Do you think he meant a stranger to come and sit in his place—to be master over all he loved? Do you think it ever entered his mind that in three little years his place would be filled by the first-comer—his daughter asked to call another man father?"

"The first-comer!" whimpered Mrs. Tempest. "Oh, this it too cruel!"

"Violet!" exclaimed Mrs. Scobel reprovingly, "when you are calmer you will be sorry for having spoken so unkindly to your dear mamma."

"I shall not be sorry for having spoken the truth," said Violet. "Mamma has heard the truth too seldom in her life. She will not hear it from Captain Winstanley—yet awhile."

And after flinging this last poisoned dart, Vixen took up the muddy skirt of her habit and left the room.

"It was rather a pity that Arion and I did not go to the bottom of that bog and stay there," she reflected. "I don't think anybody wants us above ground."

"Did you ever know anything so humiliating, so shameful, so undutiful?" demanded Mrs. Tempest piteously, as the door closed on her rebellious daughter. "What will people say if Violet is not at my wedding?"

"It would be awkward, certainly; unless there were some good reason for

17

her absence."

"People are so ill-natured. Nobody would believe in any excuse that was made. That cruel girl will disgrace me."

"She seems strongly prejudiced against Captain Winstanley. It is a great pity. But I daresay she will relent in time. If I were you, dear Mrs. Tempest, I should order the dress."

"Would you really, Fanny?"

"Yes; I should order the dress, and trust in Providence for the result. You may be able to bring her round somehow between now and the wedding."

"But I am not going to humiliate myself. I am not going to be trampled on by my daughter."

"Of course not; but you must have her at your wedding."

"If I were to tell Captain Winstanley what she has said this afternoon——"

"He would be very angry, no doubt. But I would not tell him if I were you."

"No, I shall not say anything about it."

Yet, before night, Captain Winstanley had heard every syllable that Vixen had said; with some trifling and unconscious exaggerations, hardly to be avoided by a woman of Mrs. Tempest's character, in the narration of her own wrongs.

CHAPTER III.

"I shall look like the wicked Fairy."

Nothing in Captain Winstanley's manner during the sultry summer days which went before his marriage betrayed his knowledge of Violet Tempest's rebellious spirit. He would not see that he was obnoxious to her. He spoke to her and looked at her as sweetly as if there had been the friendliest understanding between them. In all his conduct, in any act of his which approached the assumption of authority, he went to work with supreme gentleness. Yet he had his grip upon everything already, and was extending his arms in every direction, like an octopus. There were alterations being made in the garden which Violet knew were his, although Mrs. Tempest was supposed to have originated them. He had, in some measure, assumed dominion over the stables. His two hunters were already quartered there. Vixen saw them when she went her morning round with a basket of bread. They were long-bodied, hungry-looking animals; and the grooms reported them ravenous and insatiable in their feeding.

"When they've eat their corn they eats their 'ay, and when they've eat their 'ay they eats their bed, and then they takes and gnaws the wooden partitions. They'll eat up all the woodwork in the stable, before they've done. I never see such brutes," complained Bates, the head-groom.

Vixen fancied these animals were in some wise typical of their owner.

One morning when Vixen was leaning upon the half-door of Arion's loose-box, giving herself up to a quarter of an hour's petting of that much-beloved animal, Captain Winstanley came into the stable.

"Good-morning, Miss Tempest. Petting that pretty little bay of yours? I'm afraid you'll spoil him. You ought to hunt him next October."

"I shall never hunt again."

"Pshaw! At your age there's no such word as never. He's the neatest little hunter in the Forest. And on his by-days you might ride one of mine."

"Thanks," said Vixen, with a supercilious glance at the most leggy of the two hunters, "I shouldn't care to be up there. I should feel myself out of everything."

"Oh, by-the-way," said Captain Winstanley, opening the door of another loose-box, "what are we to do with this fellow?"

"This fellow" was a grand-looking bay, with herculean quarters, short legs, and a head like a war-horse. He snorted indignantly as the Captain slapped his flank, and reared his splendid crest, and seemed as if he said "Ha, ha!"

"I don't quite know of whom you are speaking when you say 'we,'" said Vixen, with an unsmiling countenance.

"Naturally of your mother and myself. I should like to include you in all our family arrangements, present or future; but you seem to prefer being left outside."

"Yes," replied Vixen, "I prefer to stand alone."

"Very well then. I repeat my question—though, as you decline to have any voice in our arrangements, it's hardly worth while to trouble you about it— what are we to do with this fellow?"

"Do with him? My father's horse!" exclaimed Vixen; "the horse he rode to his dying day! Why, keep him, of course!"

"Don't you think that is rather foolish? Nobody rides or drives him. It takes all one man's time to groom him and exercise him. You might just as well keep a white elephant in the stables."

"He was my father's favourite horse," said Vixen, with indignant tears clouding the bright hazel of her eyes; "I cannot imagine mamma capable of parting with him. Yet I ought not to say that, after my experience of the last few months," she added in an undertone.

"Well, my dear Miss Tempest, family affection is a very charming sentiment, and I can quite understand that you and your mamma would be anxious to secure your father's horse a good home and a kind master; but I cannot comprehend your mamma being so foolish as to keep a horse which is of no use to any member of her family. If the brute were of a little lighter build, I wouldn't mind riding him myself, and selling one of mine. But he's too much of a weight-carrier for me."

Vixen gave Arion a final hug, drying her angry tears upon his soft neck, and left the stable without another word. She went straight to her mother's morning-room, where the widow was sitting at a table covered with handkerchiefs-cases and glove-boxes, deeply absorbed in the study of their contents, assisted by the faithful Pauline, otherwise Polly, who had been wearing smarter gowns and caps ever since her mistress's engagement, and who was getting up a *trousseau* on her own account, in order to enter upon her new phase of existence with due dignity.

"We shall keep more company, I make no doubt, with such a gay young master as the Captain," she had observed in the confidences of Mrs. Trimmer's comfortable parlour.

"I can never bring myself to think Swedish gloves pretty," said Mrs. Tempest, as Vixen burst into the room, "but they are the fashion, and one must wear them."

"Mamma," cried Vixen, "Captain Winstanley wants you to sell Bullfinch. If you let him be sold, you will be the meanest of women."

And with this startling address Vixen left the room as suddenly as she had entered it, banging the door behind her.

Time, which brings all things, brought the eve of Mrs. Tempest's wedding. The small but perfect *trousseau*, subject of such anxious thoughts, so much study, was completed. The travelling-dresses were packed in two large oilskin-covered baskets, ready for the Scottish tour. The new travelling-bag, with monograms in pink coral on silver-gilt, a wedding present from Captain Winstanley, occupied the place of honour in Mrs. Tempest's dressing-room. The wedding-dress, of cream-coloured brocade and old point-lace, with a bonnet of lace and water-lilies, was spread upon the sofa. Everything in Mrs. Tempest's apartment bore witness to the impending change in the lady's life. Most of all, the swollen eyelids and pale cheeks of the lady, who, on this vigil of her wedding-day, had given herself up to weeping.

"Oh mum, your eyes will be so red to-morrow," remonstrated Pauline, coming into the room with another dainty little box, newly-arrived from the nearest railway-station, and surprising her mistress in tears. "Do have some red lavender. Or let me make you a cup of tea."

Mrs. Tempest had been sustaining nature with cups of tea all through the agitating day. It was a kind of drama drinking, and she was as much a slave of the teapot as the forlorn drunken drab of St. Giles's is a slave of the gin-bottle.

"Yes, you may get me another cup of tea, Pauline. I feel awfully low to-night."

"You seem so, mum. I'm sure if I didn't want to marry him, I wouldn't, if I was you. It's never too late for a woman to change her mind, not even when she's inside the church. I've known it done. I wouldn't have him, mum, if you feel your mind turn against him at the last," concluded the lady's-maid energetically.

"Not marry him, Pauline, when he is so good and noble, so devoted, so unselfish!"

Mrs. Tempest might have extended this list of virtues indefinitely, if her old servant had not pulled her up rather sharply.

"Well, mum, if he's so good and you're so fond of him, why cry?"

"You don't understand, Pauline. At such a time there are many painful feelings. I have been thinking, naturally, of my dear Edward, the best and most generous of husbands. Twenty years last June since we were married. What a child I was, Pauline, knowing nothing of the world. I had a lovely *trousseau;* but I daresay if we could see the dresses now we should think them absolutely ridiculous. And one's ideas of under-linen in those days were very limited. Those lovely satin-stitch monograms only came in when the Princess of Wales was married. Dear Edward! He was one of the handsomest men I ever saw. How could Violet believe that I should sell his favourite horse?"

"Well, mum, hearing Captain Winstanley talk about it, she naturally——"

"Captain Winstanley would never wish me to do anything I did not like."

The Captain had not said a word about Bullfinch since that morning in the stable. The noble brute still occupied his loose-box, and was fed and petted daily by Vixen, and was taken for gallops in the dry glades of the Forest, or among the gorse and heath of Boldrewood.

Mrs. Tempest had dined—or rather had not dined—in her own room on this last day of her widowhood. Captain Winstanley had business in London, and was coming back to Hampshire by the last train. There had been no settlements. The Captain had nothing to settle, and Mrs. Tempest confided in her lover too completely to desire to fence herself round with legal protections and precautions. Having only a life interest in the estate, she had nothing to leave, except the multifarious ornaments, frivolities, and luxuries which the Squire had presented to her in the course of their wedded life.

It had been altogether a trying day, Mrs. Tempest complained: in spite of the diversion to painful thought which was continually being offered by the arrival of some interesting item of the *trousseau*, elegant trifles, ordered ever so long ago, which kept dropping in at the last moment. Violet and her mother had not met during the day, and now night was hurrying on. The owls were hooting in the Forest. Their monotonous cry sounded every now and then through the evening silence like a prophesy of evil. In less than twelve hours the wedding was to take place; and as yet Vixen had shown no sign of relenting.

The dress had come from Madame Theodore's. Pauline had thrown it over a chair, with an artistic carelessness which displayed the tasteful combination of cream colour and pale azure.

Mrs. Tempest contemplated it with a pathetic countenance.

"It is simply perfect!" she exclaimed. "Theodore has a most delicate mind. There is not an atom too much blue. And how exquisitely the drapery falls! It looks as if it had been blown together. The Vandyke hat too! Violet would look lovely in it. I do not think if I were a wicked mother I should take so much pains to select an elegant costume for her. But I have always studied her dress. Even when she was in pinafores I took care that she should be picturesque. And she rewards my care by refusing to be present at my wedding. It is very cruel."

The clock struck twelve. The obscure bird clamoured a little louder in his woodland haunt. The patient Pauline, who had packed everything and arranged everything, and borne with her mistress's dolefulness all day long, began to yawn piteously.

"If you'd let me brush your hair now, ma'am," she suggested at last, "I could get to bed. I should like to be fresh to-morrow morning."

"Are you tired?" exclaimed Mrs. Tempest, wonderingly.

"Well, mum, stooping over them dress-baskets is rather tiring, and it's past twelve."

"You can go. I'll brush my hair myself."

"No, mum, I wouldn't allow that anyhow. It would make your arms ache. You ought to get to bed as soon as ever you can, or you'll look tired and 'aggard to-morrow."

That word haggard alarmed Mrs. Tempest. She would not have objected to look pale and interesting on her wedding-day, like one who had spent the previous night in tears; but haggardness suggested age; and she wanted to look her youngest when uniting herself to a husband who was her junior by some years.

So Pauline was allowed to hurry on the evening toilet. The soft pretty hair, not so abundant as it used to be, was carefully brushed; the night-lamp was lighted; and Pauline left her mistress sitting by her dressing-table in her flowing white raiment, pale, graceful, subdued in colouring, like a classic figure in a faded fresco.

She sat with fixed eyes, deep in thought, for some time after Pauline had left her, then looked uneasily at the little gem of a watch dangling on its ormolu and jasper stand. A quarter to one. Violet must have gone to bed hours ago; unless, indeed, Violet were like her mother, too unhappy to be able to sleep. Mrs. Tempest was seized with a sudden desire to see her daughter.

"How unkind of her never to come near me to say good-night, on this night of all others!" she thought, "What has she been doing all day, I wonder? Riding about the Forest, I suppose, like a wild girl, making friends of dogs and horses, and gipsies, and fox-cubs, and charcoal-burners, and all kinds of savage creatures."

And then, after a pause, she asked herself, fretfully:

"What will people say if my own daughter is not at my wedding?"

The idea of possible slander stung her sharply. She got up and walked up and down the room, inwardly complaining against Providence for using her so badly. To have such a rebellious daughter! It was sharper than a serpent's tooth.

The time had not been allowed to go by without some endeavour being made to bring Violet to a better state of feeling. That was the tone taken about

23

her by Mrs. Tempest and the Vicar's wife in their conferences. The headstrong misguided girl was to be brought to a better state of mind. Mrs. Scobel tackled her, bringing all her diplomacy to bear, but without avail. Vixen was rock. Then Mr. Scobel undertook the duty, and, with all the authority of his holy office, called upon Violet to put aside her unchristian prejudices, and behave as a meek and dutiful daughter.

"Is it unchristian to hate the man who has usurped my father's place?" Violet asked curtly.

"It is unchristian to hate anyone. And you have no right to call Captain Winstanley a usurper. You have no reason to take your mother's marriage so much to heart. There is nothing sinful, or even radically objectionable in a second marriage; though I admit that, to my mind, a woman is worthier in remaining faithful to her first love; like Anna the prophetess, who had been a widow fourscore-and-four years. Who shall say that her exceptional gift of prophecy may not have been a reward for the purity and fidelity of her life?"

Mr. Scobel's arguments were of no more effect than his wife's persuasion. His heart was secretly on Violet's side. He had loved the Squire, and he thought this marriage of Mrs. Tempest's a foolish, if not a shameful thing. There was no heartiness in the feeling with which he supervised the decoration of his pretty tittle church for the wedding.

"If she were only awake," thought Mrs. Tempest, "I would make a last appeal to her feelings, late as it is. Her heart cannot be stone."

She took her candle, and went through the dark silent house to Violet's room, and knocked gently.

"Come in," said the girl's clear voice with a wakeful sound.

"Ah!" thought Mrs. Tempest triumphantly, "obstinate as she is, she knows she is doing wrong. Conscience won't let her sleep."

Vixen was standing at her window, leaning with folded arms upon the broad wooden ledge, looking out at the dim garden, over which the pale stars were shining. There was a moon, but it was hidden by drifting clouds.

"Not in bed, Violet?" said her mother sweetly.

"No, mamma."

"What have you been doing all these hours?"

"I don't know—thinking,"

"And you never came to wish me good-night."

"I did not think you would want me. I thought you would be busy packing

24

—for your honeymoon."

"That was not kind, Violet. You must have known that I should have many painful thoughts to-night."

"I did not know it. And if it is so I can only say it is a pity the painful thoughts did not come a little sooner."

"Violet, you are as hard as iron, as cold as ice!" cried Mrs. Tempest, with passionate fretfulness.

"No, I am not, mamma; I can love very warmly, where I love deeply. I have given this night to thoughts of my dead father, whose place is to be usurped in this house from to-morrow."

"I never knew anyone so obstinately unkind. I could not have believe it possible in my own daughter. I thought you had a good heart, Violet; and yet you do not mind making me intensely wretched on my wedding-day."

"Why should you be wretched, mamma, because I prefer not to be present at your wedding? If I were there, I should be like the bad fairy at the princess's christening. I should look at everything with a malevolent eye."

Mrs. Tempest flung herself into a chair and burst into tears.

The storm of grief which had been brooding over her troubled mind all day, broke suddenly in a tempest of weeping. She could have given no reason for her distress; but all at once, on the eve of that day which was to give a new colour to her life, panic seized her, and she trembled at the step she was about to take.

"You are very cruel to me, Violet," she sobbed. "I am a most miserable woman."

Violet knelt beside her and gently took her hand, moved to pity by wretchedness so abject.

"Dear mamma, why miserable?" she asked. "This thing which you are doing is your own choice. Or, if it is not—if you have yielded weakly to over-persuasion—it is not too late to draw back. No, dear mother, even now it is not too late. Indeed, it is not. Let us run away as soon as it is light, you and I, and go off to Spain, or Italy, anywhere, leaving a letter for Captain Winstanley, to say you have changed your mind. He could not do anything to us. You have a right to draw back, even at the last."

"Don't talk nonsense, Violet," cried Mrs. Tempest peevishly. "Who said I had changed my mind? I am as devoted to Conrad as he is to me. I should be a heartless wretch if I could throw him over at the last moment. But this has been a most agitating day. Your unkindness is breaking my heart."

"Indeed, mamma, I have no wish to be unkind—not to you. But my presence at your wedding would be a lie. It would seem to give my approval to an act I hate. I cannot bring myself to do that."

"And you will disgrace me by your absence? You do not care what people may say of me."

"Nobody will care about my absence. You will be the queen of the day."

"Everybody will care—everybody will talk. I know how malicious people are, even one's most intimate friends. They will say my own daughter turned her back upon me on my wedding-day."

"They can hardly say that, when I shall be here in your house!"

Mrs. Tempest went on weeping. She had reduced herself to a condition in which it was much easier to cry than to leave off crying. The fountain of her tears seemed inexhaustible.

"A pretty object I shall look to-morrow!" she murmured plaintively, and this was all she said for some time.

Violet walked up and down the room, sorely distressed, sorely perplexed. To see her mother's grief, and to be able to give comfort, and to refuse. That must be undutiful, undaughterly, rebellious. But had not her mother forfeited all right to her obedience? Were not their hearts and lives completely sundered by this marriage of to-morrow? To Violet's stronger nature it seemed as if she were the mother—offended, outraged by a child's folly and weakness. There sat the child, weeping piteously, yearning to be forgiven. It was a complete reversal of their positions.

Her heart was touched by the spectacle of her mother's weakness, by the mute appeal of those tears.

"What does it matter to me, after all, whether I am absent or present?" she argued at last. "I cannot prevent this man coming to take possession of my father's house. I cannot hinder the outrage to my father's memory. Mamma has been very kind to me—and I have no one else in the world to love."

She took a few more turns, and then stopped by her mother's chair.

"Will it really make you happier, mamma, if I am at your wedding?"

"It will make me quite happy."

"Very well then; it shall be as you please. But, remember, I shall look like the wicked fairy. I can't help that."

"You will look lovely. Theodore has sent you home the most exquisite dress. Come to my room and try it on," said Mrs. Tempest, drying her tears, and as quickly comforted as a child who has obtained its desire by means of copious weeping.

"No, dear mamma; not to-night, I'm too tired," sighed Violet.

"Never mind, dear. Theodore always fits you to perfection. Go to bed at once, love. The dress will be a pleasant surprise for you in the morning. Good-night, pet. You have made me so happy."

"I am glad of that, mamma."

"I wish you were going to Scotland with us." (Vixen shuddered.) "I'm afraid you'll be dreadfully dull here."

"No, mamma; I shall have the dogs and horses. I shall get on very well."

"You are such a curious girl. Well, good-night, darling. You are my own Violet again."

And with this they parted; Mrs. Tempest going back to her room with restored peace of mind.

She looked at the reflection of her tear-blotted face anxiously as she paused before the glass.

"I'm afraid I shall look an object to-morrow," she said, "The morning sunshine is so searching."

CHAPTER IV.

The Vow is vowed.

Only a chosen few had been bidden to Mrs. Tempest's wedding. She had told all her friends that she meant everything to be done very quietly.

"There is so much that is saddening in my position," she said pensively. But she was resolved that those guests who were asked to lend their countenance to her espousals should be the very best people.

Lord and Lady Ellangowan had been asked, and had accepted, and their presence alone would lend dignity to the occasion. Colonel and Mrs. Carteret, from Copse Hall; the Chopnells, of Chopnell Park; and about half-a-dozen other representative landowners and commoners made up the list.

"There is such a satisfaction in knowing they are all the best people," Mrs. Tempest said to Captain Winstanley, when they went over the list together.

His own friends were but two, Major Pontorson, his best man, and a clerical cousin, with a portly figure and a portwiney nose, who was to assist Mr. Scobel in the marriage service.

It was a very pretty wedding, the neighbourhood declared unanimously; despite the absence of that most attractive feature in more youthful bridals—a string of girlish bridesmaids. The little church at Beechdale was a bower of summer flowers. The Abbey House conservatories had been emptied—the Ellangowans had sent a waggon-load of ferns and exotics. The atmosphere was heavy with the scent of yellow roses and stephanotis.

Violet stood among the guests, no gleam of colour on her cheeks except the wavering hues reflected from the painted windows in the low Gothic chancel—the ruddy gold of her hair shining under the Vandyke hat with its sweeping azure feather. She was the loveliest thing in that crowded church, whither people had come from ten miles off to see Squire Tempest's widow married; but she had a spectral look in the faint light of the chancel, and seemed as strange an image at this wedding as the ghost of Don Ramiro at Donna Clara's bridal dance, in Heine's ghastly ballad.

Violet did not look like the malevolent fairy in the old story, but she had a look and air which told everyone that this marriage was distasteful to her.

When all was over, and the register had been signed in the vestry, Captain Winstanley came up to her, with both hands extended, before all the company.

"My dear Violet, I am your father now," he said. "You shall not find me wanting in my duty."

She drew back involuntarily; and then, seeing herself the focus of so many eyes, suffered him to touch the tips of her fingers.

"You are very kind," she said. "A daughter can have but one father, and mine is dead. I hope you will be a good husband to my mother. That is all I can desire of you."

All the best people heard this speech, which was spoken deliberately, in a low clear voice, and they decided inwardly that whatever kind of wife Captain Winstanley might have won for himself, he had found his match in his stepdaughter.

Now came the ride to the Abbey House, which had put on a festive air, and where smartly-dressed servants were lending their smiles to a day which they all felt to be the end of a peaceful and comfortable era, and the beginning of an age of uncertainty. It was like that day at Versailles when the Third Estate adjourned to the Tennis Court, and the French Revolution began. People smiled, and were pleased at the new movement and expectancy in their lives, knowing not what was coming.

"We are bound to be livelier, anyhow, with a military master," said Pauline.

"A little more company in the house wouldn't come amiss, certainly," said Mrs. Trimmer.

"I should like to see our champagne cellar better stocked," remarked Forbes the butler. "We're behind the times in our sparkling wines."

Captain Winstanley entered the old oak-panelled hall with his wife on his arm, and felt himself master of such a house as a man might dream of all his life and never attain. Money could not have bought it. Taste could not have created it. The mellowing hand of time, the birth and death of many generations, had made it beautiful.

The wedding breakfast was as other wedding feasts. People ate and drank and made believe to be intensely glad, and drank more sparkling wine than was good for them at that abnormal hour, and began to feel sleepy before the speeches, brief as they were, had come to an end. The August sun shone in upon the banquet, the creams and jellies languished and collapsed in the sultry air. The wedding-cake was felt to be a nuisance. The cracker-cake exploded faintly in the languid hands of the younger guests, and those ridiculous mottoes, which could hardly amuse anyone out of Earlswood Asylum, were looked at a shade more contemptuously than usual. The weather was too warm for enthusiasm. And Violet's pale set face was almost as disheartening as the skeleton at an Egyptian banquet. When Mrs. Tempest retired to put on her travelling-dress Violet went with her, a filial attention the mother had in no wise expected.

"Dear girl," she said, squeezing her daughter's hand, "to-day is not to make the slightest difference."

"I hope not, mamma," answered Violet gravely; "but one can never tell what is in the future. God grant you may be happy!"

"I'm sure it will be my own fault if I am not happy with Conrad," said the wife of an hour, "and oh, Violet! my constant prayer will be to see you more attached to him."

Violet made no reply, and here happily Pauline brought the fawn-coloured travelling-dress, embroidered with poppies and cornflowers in their natural colours, after the style of South Kensington, a dress so distractingly lovely that it instantly put an end to serious conversation. The whole costume had been carefully thought out, a fawn-coloured parasol, edged with ostrich feathers, a fawn-coloured bonnet, fawn-coloured Hessian boots, fawn-coloured Swedish gloves with ten buttons—all prepared for the edification of railway guards and porters, and Scotch innkeepers and their *valetaille*.

Verily there are some games which seem hardly worth the candle that lights the players. And there was once upon a time an eccentric nobleman who was accounted maddest in that he made his wife dress herself from head to foot in one colour. Other times, other manners.

Violet stayed with her mother to the last, receiving the last embrace—a fond and tearful one—and watched the carriage drive away from the porch amidst a shower of rice. And then all was over. The best people were bidding her a kindly good-bye. Carriages drove up quickly, and in a quarter of an hour everyone was gone except the Vicar and his wife. Vixen found herself standing between Mr. and Mrs. Scobel, looking blankly at the hearth, where an artistic group of ferns and scarlet geraniums replaced the friendly winter fire.

"Come and spend the evening with us, dear," said Mrs. Scobel kindly; "it will be so lonely for you here."

But Violet pleaded a headache, a plea which was confirmed by her pale cheeks and the dark rings round her eyes.

"I shall be better at home," she said. "I'll come and see you in a day or two, if I may."

"Come whenever you like, dear. I wish you would come and stay with us altogether. Ignatius and I have been so pleased with your conduct to-day; and we have felt for you deeply, knowing what a conquest you have made over yourself."

The Reverend Ignatius murmured his acquiescence.

"Poor mamma!" sighed Violet, "I am afraid I have been very unkind."

And then she looked absently round the old familiar hall, and her eye lighted on the Squire's favourite chair, which still stood in its place by the hearth. Her eyes filled with sudden tears. She fancied she could see a shadowy figure sitting there. The Squire in his red coat, his long hunting whip across his knee, his honest loving face smiling at her.

She squeezed Mrs. Scobel's friendly hand, bade her and the Vicar a hurried good-bye, and ran out of the room, leaving them looking after her pityingly.

"Poor girl," said the Vicar's wife, "how keenly she feels it!"

"Ah!" sighed the Vicar, "I have never been in favour of second marriages. I can but think with St. Paul that the widow is happy if she so abide."

Vixen called Argus and went up to her room, followed by that faithful companion. When she had shut and locked the door, she flung herself on the ground, regardless of Madame Theodore's masterpiece, and clasped her arms round the dog's thick neck, and buried her face in his soft hide.

"Oh, Argus, I have not a friend in the world but you!" she sobbed.

CHAPTER V.

War to the Knife.

A strange stillness came upon the Abbey House after Mrs. Tempest's wedding. Violet received a few invitations and morning calls from friends who pitied her solitude; but the best people were for the most part away from home in August and September; some no farther than Bournemouth or Weymouth; others roaming the mountainous districts of Europe in search of the picturesque or the fashionable.

Violet did not want society. She made excuses for refusing all invitations. The solitude of her life did not afflict her. If it could have continued for ever, if Captain Winstanley and her mother could have wandered about the earth, and left her in peaceful possession of the Abbey House, with the old servants, old horses, old dogs, all things undisturbed as in her father's time, she would have been happy. It was the idea of change, a new and upstart master in her father's place, which tortured her. Any delay which kept off that evil hour was a blessed relief; but alas! the evil hour was close at hand, inevitable. That autumn proved exceptionally fine. Scotland cast aside her mantle of mist and cloud, and dressed herself in sunshine. The Trosachs blossomed as the rose. Gloomy gray glens and mountains put on an apparel of light. Mrs. Tempest wrote her daughter rapturous letters about the tour.

"We move about very slowly," she said, "so as not to fatigue me. Conrad's attention is more than words can describe. I can see that even the waiters are touched by it. He telegraphs beforehand to all the hotels, so that we have always the best rooms. He thinks nothing too good for me. It is quite saddening to see a herd of travellers sent away, houseless, every evening. The fine weather is bringing crowds to the Highlands. We could not have travelled at a more favourable time. We have had only a few showers, but in one, on Loch Katrine, my poor fawn-coloured dress suffered. The scarlet of the poppies ran into the blue of the cornflowers. Is it not a pity? I was quite unconscious of what was going on at the time; and afterwards, when I discovered it, I could have shed tears.

"I hope when you marry, darling, you will come to Scotland for your honeymoon. The mountains seem to appeal to one's highest feelings. There are ponies, too, for the ascent; which is a great comfort if one is wearing pretty boots. And you know, Violet, my idea that a woman should be essentially feminine in every detail. I never could bring myself to wear the horrid clump-soles which some women delight in. They seem to me to indicate that strong-minded and masculine character which I detest. Such women would want the suffrage, and to have the learned professions thrown open to them. I meet ladies or, at least, persons calling themselves such—in horrid waterproof costumes and with coarse cloth hats. Hideousness could go no farther. And though I regret the wreck of my fawn-colour, I can but remember with satisfaction what Theodore always says to me when she shows me one of her *chef-d'oeuvres:* 'Mrs. Tempest, it is a dress fit for a *lady.*' There are ill-natured people who declare that Theodore began life as kitchen-maid in an Irish inn, but I, for one, will never believe it. Such taste as hers indicates a refined progeniture."

With such letters as these did Mrs. Winstanley comfort her absent daughter. Vixen replied as best she might, with scraps of news about the neighbours, rich and poor, the dogs, horses, and gardens. It was hateful to her to have to direct her letters to Mrs. Winstanley.

The days went on. Vixen rode from early morning till noon, and rambled in the Forest for the best part of the afternoon. She used to take her books there, and sit for hours reading on a mossy bank under one of the boughy beeches, with Argus at her feet. The dog was company enough for her. She wanted no one better. At home the old servants were more or less—their faces always pleasant to see. Some of them had lived with her grandfather; most of them had served her father from the time he had inherited his estate. The Squire had been the most conservative and indulgent of masters; always liking to see the old faces. The butler was old, and even on his underling's bullet-head the gray hairs were beginning to show. Mrs. Trimmer was at least sixty, and had been getting annually bulkier for the last twenty years. The kitchen-maid was a comfortable-looking person of forty. There was an atmosphere of domestic peace in the offices of the Abbey House which made everybody fat. It was only by watchfulness and tight-lacing that Pauline preserved to herself that grace of outline which she spoke of in a general way as "figure."

"And what a mite of a waist I had when I first went out to service," she would say pathetically.

But Pauline was now in Scotland, harassed by unceasing cares about travelling-bags, bonnet-boxes, and extra wraps, and under-valuing Ben Nevis as not worth half the trouble that was taken to go and look at him.

The gardeners were gray-headed, and remembered potting the first fuchsia-slips that ever came to the Forest. They had no gusto for new-fangled ideas about cordon fruit-trees or root-pruning. They liked to go their own way, as their fathers and grandfathers had done before them; and, with unlimited supplies of manure, they were able to produce excellent cucumbers by the first of May, or a fair dish of asparagus by about the same time. If their produce was late it was because nature went against them. They could not command the winds, or tell the sun that he must shine. The gardens at the Abbey House were beautiful, but nature had done more for them than the Squire's old gardeners. The same rose-trees budded and bloomed year after year; the same rhododendrons and azaleas opened their big bunches of bloom. Eden could have hardly owed less to culture. The noble old cedars, the mediaeval yews, needed no gardener's hand. There was a good deal of weeding, and mowing, and rolling done from week's end to week's end; and the borders were beautified by banks of geranium and golden calceolaria, and a few other old-fashioned flowers; but scientific horticulture there was none. Some alterations had been begun under Captain Winstanley's directions; but the work languished in his absence.

It was the twentieth of September, and the travellers were expected to return within a few days—the exact date of their arrival not being announced. The weather was glorious, warmer than it had been all through the summer; and Vixen spent her life out of doors. Sad thoughts haunted her less cruelly in the great wood. There was a brightness and life in the Forest which cheered her. It was pleasant to see Argus's enjoyment of the fair weather; his wild rushes in among the underwood; his pursuit of invisible vermin under the thick holly-bushes, the brambles, and bracken; his rapturous rolling in the dewy grass, where he flung himself at full length, and rolled over and over, and leaped as if he had been revelling in a bath of freshest water; pleasant to see him race up to a serious-minded hog, and scrutinise that stolid animal closely, and then leave him to his sordid researches after edible roots, with open contempt, as who should say: "Can the same scheme of creation include me and that vulgar brute?"

All things had been set in order for the return of the newly-married couple. Mrs. Trimmer had her dinner arranged and ready to be put in hand at a moment's notice. Violet felt that the end of her peaceful life was very near. How would she bear the change? How would she be able to behave herself decently? Well, she would try her best, Heaven giving her strength. That was her last resolve. She would not make the poor frivolous mother unhappy.

"Forgive me, beloved father, if I am civil to the usurper." she said. "It will be for my mother's sake. You were always tender and indulgent to her; you would not like to see her unhappy."

These were Vixen's thoughts this bright September morning, as she sat at her lonely little breakfast-table in the sunny window of her den, with Argus by her side, intensely watchful of every morsel of bread-and-butter she ate, though he had already been accommodated with half the loaf.

She was more amiably disposed than usual this morning. She had made up her mind to make the best of a painful position.

"I shall always hate him," she told herself, meaning Captain Winstanley; "but I will begin a career of Christianlike hypocrisy, and try to make other people believe that I like him. No, Argus," as the big paw tugged her arm pleadingly, "no; now really this is sheer greediness. You can't be hungry."

A piteous whine, as of a dog on the brink of starvation, seemed to gainsay her. Just then the door opened, and the middle-aged footman entered.

"Oh, if you please, miss, Bates says would you like to see Bullfinch?"

"To see Bullfinch," echoed Vixen. "What's the matter? Is he ill? Is he hurt?"

"No, miss; but Bates thought as how maybe you'd like to see 'un before he goes away. He's sold."

Vixen turned very pale. She started up, and stood for a few moments silent, with her strong young hands clenched, just as she gripped them on the reins sometimes when Arion was running away with her and there were bogs in front.

"I'll come," she said in a half-suffocated voice.

"He has sold my father's horse, after all," she said to herself, as she went towards the stables. "Then I shall hate him openly all my life. Yes, everybody shall know that I hate him."

She found the stables in some commotion. There were two strangers, groomy-looking men, standing in front of Bullfinch's loose-box, and all the stablemen had come out of their various holes, and were standing about.

Bates looked grave and indignant.

"There isn't a finer horse in the county," he muttered; "it's a shame to send him out of it."

Vixen walked straight up to the strange men, who touched their caps, and looked at her admiringly; her dark blue cloth dress fitted her like a riding-habit, her long white throat was bare, her linen collar tied loosely with a black ribbon, her chestnut hair wound into a crown of plaits at the top of her head. The severe simplicity of her dress set off her fresh young beauty.

"She's the prettiest chestnut filly I've seen for a long time." one of the grooms said of her afterwards. "Thoroughbred to the tips of her ears."

"Who has bought this horse?" she asked authoritatively.

"My master, Lord Mallow, miss," answered the superior of the men. "You needn't be anxious about him; he'll have a rare good home."

"Will you let me see the order for taking him away?"

"Your groom has got it, miss."

Bates showed her a sheet of paper on which Captain Winstanley had written:

"Trosachs Hotel, September 12.

"The bay horse, Bullfinch, is to be delivered, with clothing, &c., to Lord Mallow's groom.

"C. WINSTANLEY."

Vixen perused this paper with a countenance full of suppressed rage.

"Does your master give much money for this horse?" she asked, turning to the strange groom.

"I haven't heard how much, miss." Of course the man knew the sum to a penny. "But I believe it's a tidyish lot."

"I don't suppose I have as much money in the world," said Vixen, "or I'd buy my father's horse of Captain Winstanley, since he is so badly in want of money, and keep him at a farm."

"I beg your pardon, miss," said the groom, "but the hoss is sold. My master has paid his money. He is a friend of Captain Winstanley's. They met somewhere in Scotland the other day and my lord bought the hoss on hearsay; and I must say I don't think he'll be disappointed in him."

"Where are you going to take him?"

"Well, it's rather an awkward journey across country. We're going to Melton. My lord is going to hunt the hoss in October, if he turns out to my lord's satisfaction."

"You are going to take him by rail?"

"Yes, miss."

"He has never been by rail in his life. It will kill him!" cried Vixen, alarmed.

"Oh no it won't, miss. Don't be frightened about him. We shall have a padded box, and everything tip-top. He'll be as snug and as tight as a sardine in its case. We'll get him to Leicestershire as fresh as paint."

Vixen went into the loose-box, where Bullfinch, all regardless of his doom, was idly munching a mouthful of upland meadow hay. She pulled down his noble head, and laid her cheek against his broad forehead, and let her tears rain on him unheeded. There was no one to see her in that dusky loose-box. The grooms were clustered at the stable-door, talking together. She was free to linger over her parting with the horse that her father had loved. She wound her arms about his arched neck, and kissed his velvet nose.

"Oh, Bullfinch, have you a memory? Will you be sorry to find yourself in a strange stable?" she asked, looking into the animal's full soft eyes with a pathetic earnestness in her own.

She dried her tears presently; she was not going to make herself a spectacle for the scornful pity of stablemen. She came out of the loose-box with a serene countenance, and went up to Lord Mallow's groom. "Please be kind to him," she said, dropping a sovereign into the man's ready hand.

"No fear of that, miss," he said; "there are very few Christians that have as good a time of it as our hosses."

That sovereign, taken in conjunction with the donor's beauty, quite vanquished Lord Mallow's stud-groom, and very nearly bought Violet Tempest a coronet.

Bullfinch was led out presently, looking like a king; but Violet did not stop to see him go away. She could hardly have borne that. She ran back to the house, put on her hat and jacket, called Argus, and set out for along ramble, to

36

walk down, if possible, the angry devil within her.

No; this she would never forgive—this sale of her father's favourite horse. It was as if some creature of her own flesh and blood had been sold into slavery. Her mother was rich, would squander hundreds on fine dresses, and would allow her dead husband's horse to be sold.

"Is Captain Winstanley such a tyrant that mamma can not prevent this shameful thing?" she asked herself. "She talks about his attention, his devotion, as if he were at her feet; and yet she suffers him to disgrace her by this unparalleled meanness!"

CHAPTER VI.

At the Kennels.

It was a fresh sunny morning, a soft west wind blowing up all the sweetness of the woods and leas. The cattle were grouped in lazy stillness on the dewy grass; the year's pigs, grown to the hobbledehoy stage of existence, were grubbing about contentedly among the furze-bushes; by the roadside, a matronly sow lay stretched flat upon her side in the sunshine, just where carriage-wheels must pass over her were carriages frequent in those parts.

Even the brightness of the morning had no charm for Vixen. There was no delight for her in the green solemnity of the forest glades, where the beechen pillars led the eye away into innumerable vistas, each grandly mysterious as a cathedral aisle. The sun shot golden arrows through dark boughs, patching the moss with translucent lights, vivid and clear as the lustre of emeralds. The gentle plash of the forest stream, rippling over its pebbly bed, made a tender music that was wont to seem passing sweet to Violet Tempest's ear. To-day she heard nothing, saw nothing. Her brain was clouded with angry thoughts.

She left the Forest by-and-by, following one of the familiar cart-tracks, and came out into the peaceful little colony of Beechdale, where it was a chance if the noonday traveller saw anything alive except a youthful family of pigs enjoying an oasis of mud in a dry land, or an intrusive dog rushing out of a cottage to salute the wayfarer with an inquiring bark. The children were still in school. The hum of their voices was wafted from the open windows. The church door stood open. The village graves upon the sunward-fronting slope were bright with common flowers; the dead lying with their feet to the west, ready to stand up and see their Lord at the resurrection morning.

Vixen hurried through the little village, not wanting to see Mrs. Scobel, or anyone she knew, this morning. There was a long rustic lane opposite the church, that led straight to the kennels.

"I will go and see the foxhounds," said Vixen. "They are true and faithful. But perhaps all those I love best have been sold, or are dead by this time."

It seemed to her ages since she had been to the kennels with her father. It had been his favourite walk, out of the hunting season, and he had rarely suffered a week to pass without making his visit of inspection. Since her return Violet had carefully avoided the well-known spot; but to-day, out of the very bitterness of her heart, came a desire to renew past associations. Bullfinch was gone for ever, but the hounds at least remained; and her father had loved them almost as well as he had loved Bullfinch.

Nothing was changed at the kennels. The same feeder in corduroy and fustian came out of the cooking-house when Vixen opened the five-barred gate. The same groom was lounging in front of the stables, where the horses were kept for the huntsman and his underlings. The whole place had the same slumberous out-of-season look she remembered so well of old in the days when hunting was over.

The men touched their caps to Miss Tempest as she passed them. She went straight to the kennels. There were the three wooden doors, opening into three square stone-paved yards, each door provided with a small round eye-hole, through which the authorities might scrutinise the assembly within. A loud yelping arose as Vixen's footsteps drew near. Then there were frantic snuffings under the doors, and a general agitation. She looked through the little eye-hole into the middle yard. Yes; there they were, fourteen or fifteen couple, tumultuously excited, as if they knew she was there: white and black and tan, pointed noses, beautiful intelligent eyes, bright tan spots upon marked brows, some with a streak of white running down the long sharp noses, some heavy in the jowl, some with muzzles sharp as a greyhound's, thirty tails erect and agitated.

The feeder remembered Miss Tempest perfectly, though it was more than three years since her last visit.

"Would you like to go in and see 'em, miss?" he said.

"Yes, if you please, Dawson. You have Gauntlet still, I see. That is Gauntlet, isn't it? And Dart, and Juno, and Ringlet, and Artful?"

"Yes, miss. There ain't many gone since you was here. But there's a lot o' poppies. You'd like to see the poppies, wouldn't you, miss? They be in the next kennel, if you'll just wait five minutes."

Cleanliness was the order of the day at the kennels, but to do the late master's daughter more honour, Dawson the feeder called a bright-looking lad, his subordinate, and divers pails of water were fetched, and the three little yards washed out vigorously before Miss Tempest was invited to enter. When she did go in, the yard was empty and clean as a new pin. The hounds had been sent into their house, where they were all grouped picturesquely on a bench littered with straw, looking as grave as a human parliament, and much wiser. Nothing could be more beautiful than their attitudes, or more intelligent than their countenances.

Vixen looked in at them through the barred window.

"Dear things," she exclaimed; "they are as lovely as ever. How fond papa was of them."

And then the kennel-huntsman, who had appeared on the scene by this time, opened the door and smacked his whip; and the fifteen couple came leaping helter-skelter out into the little yard, and made a rush at Vixen, and surrounded her, and fawned upon her, and caressed her as if their recognition of her after long years was perfect, and as if they had been breaking their hearts for her in the interval. Perhaps they would have been just as affectionate to the next comer, having a large surplus stock of love always on hand ready to be lavished on the human race; but Vixen took these demonstrations as expressive of a peculiar attachment, and was moved to tears by the warmth of this canine greeting.

"Thank God! there are some living things that love me," she exclaimed.

"Something that loves you!" cried a voice from the door of the yard. "Does not everything noble or worthy love you, as it loves all that is beautiful?"

Turning quickly, with a scared look, Violet saw Roderick Vawdrey standing in the doorway.

He stood quietly watching her, his dark eyes softened with a look of tender admiration. There could hardly have been a prettier picture than the tall girlish figure and bright chestnut head, the fair face bending over the upturned noses of the hounds as they clustered round her, some standing up with their strong white paws upon her shoulder, some nestling at her knees. Her hat had fallen off, and was being trampled under a multitude of restless feet.

Rorie came into the little yard. The huntsman cracked his whip, and the hounds went tumbling one over the other into their house, where they leaped upon their straw bed, and grouped themselves as if they had been sitting for their portraits to Sir Edwin Landseer. Two inquisitive fellows stood up with their paws upon the ledge of the barred window, and looked out at Violet and the new master.

"I did not know you were at Briarwood," she said, as they shook hands.

"I only came home last night. My first visit was naturally here. I wanted to see if everything was in good order."

"When do you begin to hunt?"

"On the first of October. You are going to be amongst us this year, of course."

"No. I have never followed the hounds since papa's death. I don't suppose I ever shall again."

"What, not with your stepfather?"

"Certainly not with Captain Winstanley."

"Then you must marry a hunting-man," said Rorie gaily. "We can't afford to lose the straightest rider in the Forest."

"I am not particularly in love with hunting—for a woman. There seems something bloodthirsty in it. And Bates says that if ladies only knew how their horses' backs get wrung in the hunting season, they would hardly have the heart to hunt. It was very nice to ride by papa's side when I was a little girl. I would have gone anywhere with him—through an Indian jungle after tigers—but I don't care about it now."

"Well, perhaps you are right; though I should hardly have expected such mature wisdom from my old playfellow, whose flowing locks used once to be the cynosure of the hunting-field. And now, Violet—I may call you Violet, may I not, as I did in the old days?—at least, when I did not call you Vixen."

"That was papa's name," she said quickly. "Nobody ever calls me that now."

"I understand; I am to call you Violet. And we are to be good friends always, are we not, with a true and loyal friendship?"

"I have not so many friends that I can afford to give up one who is stanch and true," answered Violet sadly.

"And I mean to be stanch and true, believe me; and I hope, by-and-by, when you come to know Mabel, you and she will be fast friends. You may not cotton to her very easily at first, because, you see, she reads Greek, and goes in for natural science, and has a good many queer ways. But she is all that is pure-minded and noble. She has been brought up in an atmosphere of adulation, and that has made her a little self-opinionated. It is the only fault she has."

"I shall be very glad if she will let me like her," Violet said meekly.

They had strolled away from the kennels into the surrounding forest, where the free horses of the soil were roaming from pasture to pasture, and a few vagabond pigs were stealing a march on their brethren, for whom the joys of pannage-time had not yet begun. They walked along idly, following a cart-track that led into the woody deeps where the earliest autumn leaves were dropping gently in the soft west wind. By-and-by they came to a fallen oak, lying by the side of the track, ready for barking, and it seemed the most natural thing in the world to sit down side by side on this rustic seat, and talk of days gone by, lazily watching the flickering shadows and darting sunrays in the opposite thicket, or along the slanting stretch of open turf—that smooth emerald grass, so inviting to the eye, so perilous to the foot of man or beast.

"And now, Violet, tell me all about yourself, and about this second marriage of your mother's," Roderick began earnestly; "I hope you have quite reconciled yourself to the idea of it by this time."

"I have not reconciled myself; I never shall," answered Violet, with restrained anger. "I know that mamma has heaped up sorrow for herself in the days to come, and I pity her too much to be angry with her. Yes; I, who ought to look up to and respect my mother, can only look down upon her and pity her. That is a hard thing, is it not, Rorie? She has married a bad man—mean, and false—and tyrannical. Shall I tell you what he has done within these last few days?"

"Do. I hope it is not anything very bad."

Violet told how Bullfinch had been sold.

"It looks mean, certainly," said Mr. Vawdrey; "but I daresay to Captain Winstanley, as a man of the world, it might seem a foolish thing to keep a horse nobody rode; especially such a valuable horse as Bullfinch. Your father gave two hundred and fifty for him at Andover, I remember. And you really have too many horses at the Abbey House."

"Arion will be the next to be sold, I daresay."

"Oh, no, no. He could not be such an insolent scoundrel as to sell your horse. That would be too much. Besides, you will be of age in a year or two, and your own mistress."

"I shall not be of age for the next seven years. I am not to come of age till I am five-and-twenty."

"Phew!" whistled Rorie, "That's a long shot off. How is that?"

41

"Papa left it so in his will. It was his care of me, no doubt. He never would have believed that mamma would marry again."

"And for the next seven years you are to be in a state of tutelage, dependent on your mother for everything?"

"For everything. And that will really mean dependent upon Captain Winstanley; because I am very sure that as long as he lets mamma wear pretty dresses and drink orange pekoe out of old china, she will be quite contented to let him be master of everything else."

"But if you were to marry——"

"I suppose that would entangle or disentangle matters somehow. But I am not likely to marry."

"I don't see that," said Rorie. "I should think nothing was more likely."

"Allow me to be the best judge of my own business," exclaimed Vixen, looking desperately angry. "I will go so far as to say that I never shall marry."

"Oh, very well, if you insist upon it, let it be understood so. And now, Vix ——Violet, don't you think if you could bring yourself to conciliate Captain Winstanley—to resign yourself, in fact, to the inevitable, and take things pleasantly, it would make your life happier for the next seven years? I really would try to do it, if I were you."

"I had made up my mind to an existence of hypocrisy before he sold Bullfinch," replied Vixen, "but now I shall hate him frankly."

"But, Violet, don't you see that unless you can bring yourself to live pleasantly with that man your life will be made miserable? Fate condemns you to live under the same roof with him."

"I am not sure about that. I could go out as a governess. I am not at all clever, but I think I could teach as much as would be good value for twenty pounds a year; or at the worst I might give my services in exchange for a comfortable home, as the advertisements say. How I wish I could read Greek and play Chopin, like Lady Mabel Ashbourne. I'll write to dear old McCroke, and ask her to get me a place."

"My dear Violet, how can you talk so absurdly. You, the future mistress of the Abbey House—you, with your youth and beauty and high spirit—to go meandering about the world teaching buttermen's or tea-dealers' children to spell B a, ba, and A b, ab?"

"It might be better than sitting at meat with a man I detest," said Vixen. "Am I to value the flesh-pots of Egypt more than my liberty and independence of mind?"

"You have your mother to think of," urged Roderick. "You owe duty and obedience to her, even if she has offended you by this foolish marriage. If you have so bad an opinion of Captain Winstanley, you are all the more bound to stand by your mother."

"That is an argument worth listening to," said Vixen. "It might be cruel to leave poor mamma quite at his mercy. I don't suppose he would actually ill-treat her. He knows his own interest too well for that. He would not lock her up in a cellar, or beat, or starve her. He will be content with making himself her master. She will have no more will of her own than if she were a prettily dressed doll placed at the head of the table for show. She will be lulled into a state of childish bliss, and go smiling through life, believing she has not a wish ungratified. Everybody will think her the happiest of women, and Captain Winstanley the best of husbands."

Vixen said all this with prophetic earnestness, looking straight forward into the green glade before her, where the beech-nuts and acorns were dropping in a gentle rain of plenty.

"I hope things won't be quite so bad as you anticipate. I hope you will be able to make yourself happy, in spite of Captain Winstanley. And we shall see each other pretty often, I hope, Violet, as we used in old times. The Dovedales are at Wiesbaden; the Duke only holds existence on the condition of deluging himself with German waters once a year; but they are to be back early in November. I shall make the Duchess call on Mrs. Winstanley directly she returns."

"Thanks; mamma will be very pleased. I wonder you are not with them."

"Oh, I had to begin my duties as M. F. H. I wouldn't have been away for the world."

Violet looked at her watch. It was a good deal later than she had supposed. Time goes quickly when one is talking over a new grievance with an old friend. She was a long way from the Abbey House.

"I must go home," she said; "mamma and Captain Winstanley may arrive at any moment. There is no time named in mamma's last telegram; she said only that they are moving gently homewards."

"Let us go then," said Rorie, rising from his rugged seat.

"But I am not going to take you out of your way. Every step of my journey home takes you further from Briarwood."

"Never mind if it does. I mean to walk to the Abbey House with you. I daresay, if I were very tired, Bates would lend me a mount home."

43

"You can have Arion, if you like."

"No, thanks. Arion shall not have my thirteen stone; I want a little more timber under me."

"You ought to have had Bullfinch," said Vixen regretfully.

"I would have had him, if I had known he was in the market. The writing of a figure or so more or less on a cheque should not have hindered me."

CHAPTER VII.

A Bad Beginning.

That walk through the Forest was very pleasant to Violet. It was a day on which mere existence was a privilege; and now that her spirits had been soothed by her confidential talk with Rorie, Vixen could enjoy those sights and sounds and sweet wild scents of the woodland that had ever been a rapture to her.

This Forest-born girl loved her native woods as Wordsworth loved his lakes and mountains, as Byron loved the bleak bare landscape round the city of Aberdeen. Their poetry and beauty filled her heart with a deep contentment. To walk or ride alone through pathless forest glades, or in the scented darkness of fir plantations, was enough for happiness. But it was comforting to-day—on this day when her heart had been so cruelly wounded —to have Roderick Vawdrey by her side. It was like a leaf out of the closed volume of the past.

They talked freely and happily during that long homewards walk, and their conversation was chiefly of bygone days. Almost every speech began with "Do you remember?" Vixen was gayer than she had been for a long time, save once or twice, when a pang shot through her heart at the idea that Bullfinch was being shaken about in a railway-box, oscillating helplessly with every vibration of the train, and panic-stricken in every tunnel.

The sun had declined from his meridian; he had put on his sober afternoon glory, and was sending shafts of mellower gold along the green forest aisles, when Miss Tempest and her companion drew near the Abbey House. They went in at the gate by the keeper's cottage, the gate which Titmouse had jumped so often in the days when he carried his childish mistress. They went through the wood of rhododendrons, and past the old archway leading to the stables, and round by the shrubbery to the porch. The door stood open as usual, and the Squire's old pointer was lying on the threshold; but within all was commotion. Dress-baskets, hat-cases, bonnet-boxes, gun-cases, travelling-bags, carriage-rugs, were lying about in every direction. Mrs. Winstanley was leaning back in the large chair by the fireplace, fanning herself with her big black fan; Pauline was standing by in attendance; and the silver tray, with the Swansee tea-set, was being brought in by Forbes the butler, whose honest old face wore a troubled aspect.

Captain Winstanley was standing with his back to the hearth, his countenance and whole figure wearing the unmistakable air of the master of a house who has returned to his domicile in an execrable temper.

Violet ran to Mrs. Winstanley, every other thought forgotten in the pleasure of seeing her mother again. These three weeks were the longest parting mother and daughter had ever known; and after all, blood is thicker than water; and there is a natural leaning in a child's mind even to the weakest of parents.

Mr. Vawdrey stood in the background, waiting till those affectionate greetings natural to such an occasion should be over.

But to his surprise there were no such greetings. Mrs. Winstanley went on fanning herself vehemently, with a vexed expression of countenance, while Violet bent over and kissed her. Captain Winstanley swayed himself slowly backwards and forwards upon the heels of his boots, and whistled to himself sotto voce, with his eyes fixed upon some lofty region of empty air. He vouchsafed not the faintest notice of his stepdaughter or Mr. Vawdrey.

"It's really too bad of you, Violet," the mother exclaimed at last.

"Dear mamma," cried Vixen, in blank amazement, "what have I done?"

"To go roaming about the country," pursued Mrs. Winstanley plaintively, "for hours at a stretch, nobody knowing where to find you or what had become of you. And my telegram lying there unattended to."

"Did you telegraph, mamma?"

"Did I telegraph? Should I come home without telegraphing? Should I be so mad as to expose myself knowingly to the outrage which has been offered to me to-day?"

"Dearest mamma, you alarm me. What has happened?"

"One of the deepest humiliations I ever had to endure. But you were roaming about the Forest. You were following the instincts of your wild

45

nature. What do you care for my mortification? If I had telegraphed to my housekeeper, it would not have happened. But I trusted in my daughter."

"Dear mamma," pleaded Vixen, looking anxious and bewildered, "if you would only explain. You make me miserable. What has happened?"

"Violet, your stepfather and I had to drive home from the station in a fly!"

"Oh, mamma!" cried Vixen, with a gasp. "Is that all?"

"Is that all? Do you think that is not enough? Do you understand, child?— a fly—a common innkeeper's fly—that anybody may have for half-a-guinea; a fly with a mouldy lining, smelling of—other people! And on such an occasion, when every eye was upon us! No; I was never so degraded. And we had to wait—yes, a quarter of an hour, at least, and it seemed ages, while Pycroft's fly was got ready for us; yes, while a rough forest pony was dragged out of his wretched stable, and a man, whose face had not been washed for a week, shuffled himself into an old coachman's coat. And there were all the porters staring at me, and laughing inwardly, I know. And, as a last drop in the cup, Colonel Carteret drove up in his phaeton to catch the up-train just as we were getting into that disgraceful looking vehicle, and would stop to shake hands with us both, and insisted upon handing me into the horrid thing."

"Dear mamma, I am more sorry than I can say," said Vixen gently; "but I was afraid it was something much worse."

"Nothing could be worse, Vixen."

"Then the telegram was to order the carriage to meet you, I suppose?"

"Of course. We telegraphed from the Grosvenor at nine o'clock this morning. Who would imagine that you would be out of doors at such an hour?"

"I am not often out so early. But something happened this morning to put me out of temper, and I went for a ramble."

"A ramble lasting from ten in the morning till half-past four in the afternoon," remarked Captain Winstanley, with his gaze still fixed upon empty space. "Rather a long walk for a solitary young lady."

Vixen appeared unconscious that anyone had spoken. Roderick Vawdrey felt a burning desire to kick the new master of the Abbey House.

"Shall I pour out your tea, mamma?" asked Vixen meekly.

"If you like. I am utterly prostrate. To have no carriage to meet me on such an occasion! I daresay everybody in the Forest knows all about it by this time. When I came home from my honeymoon with your poor papa, the joy-bells rang all the afternoon, and the road was lined with people waiting to get a glimpse of us, and there were floral arches——"

"Ah, mamma, those things cannot happen twice in a lifetime," said Vixen, with irrepressible bitterness. "One happy marriage is as much as any woman can expect."

"A woman has the right to expect her own carriage," said Captain Winstanley.

"I am afraid I have paid my visit at rather at unfortunate moment," said Roderick, coming forward and addressing himself solely to Mrs. Winstanley; "but I could not go without saying How do you do? I hope you had a pleasant journey from Scotland—bar the fly."

"How do you do, Roderick? Yes; it was all pleasant except that last contretemps. Imagine the Duchess of Dovedale's feelings if she arrived at the station adjoining her own estate, and found no carriage to meet her!"

"My aunt would tuck up her petticoats and trudge home," answered Roderick, smiling. "She's a plucky little woman."

"Yes, perhaps on an ordinary occasion. But to-day it was so different. Everybody will talk about our return."

"Most people are still away," suggested Rorie, with a view to comfort.

"Oh, but their servants will hear it, and they will tell their masters and mistresses. All gossip begins that way. Besides, Colonel Carteret saw us, and what he knows everybody knows."

After this, Roderick felt that all attempts at consolation were hopeless. He would have liked to put Mrs. Winstanley into a better temper, for Violet's sake. It was not a pleasant home atmosphere in which he was obliged to leave his old playfellow on this the first day of her new life. Captain Winstanley maintained a forbidding silence; Mrs. Winstanley did not even ask anyone to have a cup of tea; Violet sat on the opposite side of the hearth, pale and quiet, with Argus at her knee, and one arm wound caressingly round his honest head.

"I've been inspecting the kennels this morning," said Roderick, looking at the new master of the Abbey House with a cheerful assumption that everything was going on pleasantly. "We shall begin business on the first. You'll hunt, of course?"

"Well, yes; I suppose I shall give myself a day occasionally."

"I shall not have a happy moment while you are out," said Mrs. Winstanley. "I used to be miserable about poor dear Edward."

Vixen winced. These careless references to the dead hurt her more than the silence of complete oblivion. To remember, and to be able to speak so lightly. That seemed horrible.

"I doubt if I shall hunt much this season," pursued Captain Winstanley, as much as to say that he was not going to be grateful to the new master of the foxhounds as a public benefactor, however many hundreds that gentleman might disburse in order to make up the shortcomings of a scanty subscription. "I shall have a great deal to occupy me. This place has been much neglected —naturally—within the last few years. There is no end of work to be done."

"Are you going to pull down the Abbey House and build an Italian villa on its site?" asked Vixen, her upper lip curling angrily. "That would be rather a pity. Some people think it a fine old place, and it has been in my father's family since the reign of Henry the Eighth."

To the Captain's ear this speech had a covert insolence. The Abbey House was to belong to Violet in the future. Neither he nor his wife had a right to touch a stone of it. Indeed, it was by no means clear to him that there might not be ground for a Chancery suit in his cutting down a tree.

"I hope I shall do nothing injudicious," he said politely.

"My aunt will be back in a week or two, Mrs. Winstanley," said Roderick. "I shall bring her over to see you directly she settles down at Ashbourne. And now I think I'd better be off; I've a long walk home, and you must be too tired to care about talking or being talked to."

"I am very tired," answered Mrs. Winstanley languidly; "but I should have liked to hear all your news."

"I'm afraid that's not much. I only came home last night; I have been shooting grouse in Renfrew."

"Plenty of birds this year?" inquired the Captain, with a languid interest.

"Pretty fair. The rainy spring killed a good many of the young birds."

"Do you remember any year in which that complaint was not made?" retorted Captain Winstanley.

Rorie took his departure after this, and contrived to give Violet's hand an encouraging squeeze at parting, accompanied with a straight steady look, which said as plainly as words: "You have one friend who will be stanch and true, come what may."

Vixen understood him, and sudden tears welled up to her eyes—the first that had clouded them since her parting with Bullfinch. She brushed them away hurriedly, but not so quickly as to escape Captain Winstanley's observation.

"If you'll excuse me, mamma. I'll run and dress for dinner," she said, "unless there is anything I can do for you. Your rooms are quite ready."

"I'm glad of that," replied Mrs. Winstanley fretfully; "for really after our reception at the railway-station, I expected to find everything at sixes and sevens."

"Dear mamma, you must know that was quite an accident."

"An accident very likely to occur when a young lady indulges in tête-à-tête forest rambles with an old friend, instead of waiting at home for her mother's letters and telegrams," remarked Captain Winstanley, caressing his neat whisker with his irreproachable hand.

"What do you mean?" said Vixen, turning sharply upon him. "I went out alone this morning. Mr. Vawdrey and I met at the kennels by accident."

"A chapter of accidents," sneered the Captain. "I have no objection to make, Miss Tempest, if your mamma has none. But I am rather sorry for the young lady Mr. Vawdrey is going to marry."

"Mr. Vawdrey was my father's friend, and will never cease to be mine," said Vixen, with flashing eyes. "There can be nothing offensive to Lady Mabel Ashbourne in our friendship."

She was gone before her stepfather could reply, or her mother reprove her want of respect for that new relative.

"I suppose I had better go and dress too," said Mrs. Winstanley, "and in the evening we can talk about our first dinner-party. I daresay we shall have a great many people calling to-morrow afternoon. It will be rather trying. There is such a painful feeling in being a bride and not a bride, as it were. People's congratulations hardly sound hearty."

"I daresay they have rather a vapid flavour, like a warmed-up dinner," said the Captain. "That is the result of living in a neighbourhood where your first husband was known and popular. If we went among strangers, their congratulations would be a great deal heartier. But I hope you don't begin to repent already, my dear Pamela."

"Conrad! How can you imagine such a thing?—after your delicate attentions, your devoted care of me during our tour. What dress shall I wear this evening? Do you like me best in blue or amber?"

"To my eye all colours suit you. But I think a woman"—he was going to say "of your age," but checked himself and substituted—"in the maturity of her beauty looks best in velvet, or some rich and heavy material that falls in massive folds, like the drapery in a portrait by Velasquez. A border of fur, too, is an artistic introduction in a woman's dress—you see it often in Velasquez. Heavy old laces are, of course, always admirable. And for colour I like the warmer hues best—wine-dark purples or deep glowing reds; rich ruddy browns, with a knot of amber now and then for relief."

"How beautifully you talk," cried Mrs. Winstanley, delighted. "I only wish Theodore could hear you. It would give her new ideas; for, after all, the best dressmakers are *bornées*. It is too early in the year for velvet. I shall put on my dark green brocade with the old Flanders lace. I am so glad you like lace. It is my chief weakness. Even dear Edward, who was so generous, thought me a little extravagant in the matter of lace. But when one once begins to collect, the study is so interesting. One is led on."

"Good Heavens! is my wife a collector?" thought Captain Winstanley, horrified. "That must be put a stop to, or she will ruin me."

And then he went off to his dressing-room rather wearily, to put on full-dress for a home dinner, a sacrifice to his new state of existence which he found very irksome. He would have liked to dine in a shooting-jacket, and smoke all the evening. But his smoking now, instead of pervading the whole house, as it had done in his snug bachelor quarters, was an indulgence to be taken out of doors, or in a room appointed for the purpose. He was not even to smoke in the fine old hall, for it was one of the family sitting-rooms, and Mrs. Winstanley could not endure smoke.

"I am not at all fanciful or capricious," she told her husband early in the honeymoon, "but smoking is one of my horrors. I hope, dear Conrad, it is not too much to ask you never to smoke in any room I use."

Captain Winstanley pledged himself to respect this and every other wish of his wife's. It was his policy to be subservient in small matters, in order to be master in essentials. But that daily dressing for dinner was something of a bore; and the dinners themselves—*tête-à-tête* dinners, in which he had to take as much trouble to be amusing as at a dinner-party, had been apt to hang heavily upon him. He had even proposed dining at the *table-d'hôte*, while they were on their Scotch travels, but this idea Mrs. Winstanley rejected with horror.

"I have never dined at a *table-d'hôte* in my life, Conrad," she exclaimed, "and I certainly should not begin during my wedding tour."

CHAPTER VIII.

On Half Rations.

Captain Winstanley entered upon his new position with a fixed determination to make the best of it, and with a very clear view of its advantages and disadvantages. For seven years he was to be master of everything—or his wife was to be mistress, which, in his mind, was exactly the same. No one could question his use of the entire income arising from Squire Tempest's estates during that period. When Violet came of age—on her twenty-fifth birthday—the estates were to be passed over to her *in toto;* but there was not a word in the Squire's will as to the income arising during her minority. Nor had the Squire made any provision in the event of his daughter's marriage. If Violet were to marry to-morrow, she would go to her husband penniless. He would not touch a sixpence of her fortune until she was twenty-five. If she were to die during her minority the estate would revert to her mother.

It was a very nice estate, taken as a sample of a country squire's possessions. Besides the New Forest property, there were farms in Wiltshire and Dorsetshire; the whole yielding an income of between five and six thousand a year. With such a revenue, and the Abbey House and all its belongings rent free, Captain Winstanley felt himself in a land of Canaan. But then there was the edict that seven years hence he was to go forth from this land of milk and honey; or, at any rate, was to find himself living at the Abbey House on a sorely restricted income. Fifteen hundred a year in such a house would mean genteel beggary, he told himself despondently. And even this genteel beggary would be contingent on his wife's life. Her death would rob him of everything.

He had a mind given to calculation, and he entered upon the closest calculations as to his future. He meant to enjoy life, of course. He had always done that to the best of his ability. But he saw that the chief duty he owed to himself was to save money; and to lay by against the evil inevitable day when Violet Tempest would despoil him of power and wealth. The only way to do this was by the cutting down of present expenses, and an immediate narrowing of the lines on which the Abbey House was being conducted; for the Captain had discovered that his wife, who was the most careless and incompetent of women as regards money matters, had been spending the whole of her income since her husband's death. If she had not spent her money on society, she had spent it on travelling, on lace, on old china, on dress, on hothouse flowers, on a stable which was three times larger than she could possibly require, on a household in which there were a good many more cats than were wanted to catch mice, on bounties and charities that were given upon no principle, not even from inclination, but only because Squire Tempest's widow had never been able to say No.

Captain Winstanley's first retrenchment had been the sale of Bullfinch, for which noble animal Lord Mallow, a young Irish viscount, had given a cheque for three hundred guineas. This money the Captain put on deposit at his banker's, by way of a nest-egg. He meant his deposit account to grow into something worth investing before those seven fat years were half gone.

He told his wife his views on the financial question one morning when they were breakfasting *tête-à-tête* in the library, where the Squire and his family had always dined when there was no company. Captain and Mrs. Winstanley generally had the privilege of breakfasting alone, as Violet was up and away before her mother appeared. The Captain also was an early riser, and had done half his day's work before he sat down to the luxurious nine-o'clock breakfast with his wife.

"I have been thinking of your ponies, pet," he said, in a pleasant voice, half careless, half caressing, as he helped himself to a salmon cutlet. "Don't you think it would be a very wise thing to get rid of them?"

"Oh, Conrad!" cried his wife, letting the water from the urn overflow the teapot in her astonishment; "you can't mean that! Part with my ponies?"

"My dear love, how often do you drive them in a twelvemonth?"

"Not very often, perhaps. I have felt rather nervous driving lately—carts and great waggon-loads of hay come out upon one so suddenly from cross-roads. I don't think the waggoners would care a bit if one were killed. But I am very fond of my gray ponies. They are so pretty. They have quite Arabian heads. Colonel Carteret says so, and he has been in Arabia."

"But, my dear Pamela, do you think it worth while keeping a pair of ponies because they are pretty, and because Colonel Carteret, who knows about as much of a horse as I do of a megalosaurus says they have Arabian heads? Have you ever calculated what those ponies cost you?"

"No, Conrad; I should hate myself if I were always calculating the cost of things."

"Yes, that's all very well in the abstract. But if you are inclined to waste money, it's just as well to know how much you are wasting. Those ponies are costing you at the least one hundred and fifty pounds a year, for you could manage with a man less in the stables if you hadn't got them."

"That's a good deal of money certainly," said Mrs. Winstanley, who hated driving, and had only driven her ponies because other people in her position drove ponies, and she felt it was a right thing to do.

Still the idea of parting with anything that appertained to her state wounded her deeply.

"I can't see why we should worry ourselves about the cost of the stables," she said; "they have gone on in the same way ever since I was married. Why should things be different now?"

"Don't you see that you have the future to consider, Pamela. This handsome income which you are spending so lavishly——"

"Edward never accused me of extravagance," interjected Mrs. Winstanley tearfully, "except in lace. He did hint that I was a little extravagant in lace."

"This fine income is to be reduced seven years hence to fifteen hundred a year, an income upon which—with mine added to it—you could not expect to be able to carry on life decently in such a house as this. So you see, Pamela, unless we contrive between us to put by a considerable sum of money before your daughter's majority, we shall be obliged to leave the Abbey House, and live in a much smaller way than we are living now."

"Leave the Abbey House!" cried Mrs. Winstanley with a horrified look. "Conrad, I have lived in this house ever since I was married."

"Am I not aware of that, my dear love? But, all the same, you would have to let this place, and live in a much smaller house, if you had only fifteen hundred a year to live upon."

"It would be too humiliating! At the end of one's life. I should never survive such a degradation."

"It may be prevented if we exercise reasonable economy during the next seven years."

"Sell my ponies, then, Conrad; sell them immediately. Why should we allow them to eat us out of house and home. Frisky shies abominably if she is in the least bit fresh, and Peter has gone so far as to lie down in the road when he has had one of his lazy fits."

"But if they are really a source of pleasure to you, my dear Pamela, I should hate myself for selling them," said the Captain, seeing he had gained his point.

"They are not a source of pleasure. They have given me some awful frights."

"Then we'll send them up to Tattersall's immediately, with the carriage."

"Violet uses the carriage with Titmouse." objected Mrs. Winstanley. "We could hardly spare the carriage."

"My love, if I part with your ponies from motives of economy, do you suppose I would keep a pony for your daughter?" said the Captain with a grand air. "No; Titmouse must go, of course. That will dispose of a man and a boy in the stables. Violet spends so much of her life on horseback, that she cannot possibly want a pony to drive."

"She is very fond of Titmouse," pleaded the mother.

"She has a tendency to lavish her affection on quadrupeds—a weakness which hardly needs fostering. I shall write to Tattersall about the three ponies this morning; and I shall send up that great raking brown horse Bates rides at the same time. Bates can ride one of my hunters. That will bring down the stable to five horses—my two hunters, Arion, and your pair of carriage-horses."

"Five horses," sighed Mrs. Winstanley pensively; "I shall hardly know those great stables with only five horses in them. The dear old place used to look so pretty and so full of life when I was first married, and when the Squire used to coax me to go with him on his morning rounds. The horses used to move on one side, and turn their heads so prettily at the sound of his voice— such lovely, sleek, shining creatures, with big intelligent eyes."

"You would be a richer woman if it had not been for those lovely, sleek, shining creatures," said Captain Winstanley. "And now, love, let us go round the gardens, and you will see the difference that young able-bodied gardeners are making in the appearance of the place."

Mrs. Winstanley gave a plaintive little sigh as she rose and rang the bell for Pauline. The good old gray-haired gardeners—the men who had seemed to her as much a part of the gardens as the trees that grew in them—these hoary and faithful servants had been cashiered, to make room for two brawny young Scotchmen, whose dialect was as Greek to the mistress of the Abbey House. It wounded her not a little to see these strangers at work in her grounds. It gave an aspect of strangeness to her very life out of doors. She hardly cared to go into her conservatories, or to loiter on her lawn, with those hard unfamiliar eyes looking at her. And it wrung her heart to think of the Squire's old servants thrust out in their old age, unpensioned, uncared for. Yet this was a change that had come about with her knowledge, and, seemingly, with her consent. That is to say, the Captain had argued her into a corner, where she stood, like the last forlorn king in a game of draughts, fenced round and hemmed in by opponent kings. She had not the strength of mind to assert herself boldly, and say: "I will not have it so. This injustice shall not be."

A change had come over the spirit of the Abbey House kitchen, which was sorely felt in Beechdale and those half-dozen clusters of cottages within a two-mile radius, which called themselves villages, and all of which had turned to the Abbey House for light and comfort, as the sunflower turns to the sun. Captain Winstanley had set his face against what he called miscellaneous charity. Such things should be done and no other. His wife should subscribe liberally to all properly organised institutions—schools, Dorcas societies, maternity societies, soup-kitchens, regulated dole of bread or coals, every form of relief that was given systematically and by line and rule; but the good Samaritan business—the picking up stray travellers, and paying for their maintenance at inns—was not in the Captain's view of charity. Henceforward Mrs. Winstanley's name was to appear with due honour upon all printed subscription-lists, just as it had done when she was Mrs. Tempest; but the glory of the Abbey House kitchen had departed. The beggar and the cadger were no longer sure of a meal. The villagers were no longer to come boldly asking for what they wanted in time of trouble—broth, wine, jelly, for the sick, allowances of new milk, a daily loaf when father was out of work, broken victuals at all times. It was all over. The kitchen-doors were to be closed against all intruders.

"My love, I do not wonder that you have spent every sixpence of your income," said Captain Winstanley. "You have been keeping an Irish household. I can fancy an O'Donoghue or a Knight of Glyn living in this kind of way; but I should hardly have expected such utter riot and recklessness in an English gentleman's house."

"I am afraid Trimmer has been rather extravagant," assented Mrs. Winstanley. "I have trusted everything to her entirely, knowing that she is quite devoted to us, poor dear soul."

"She is so devoted, that I should think in another year or so, at the rate she was going, she would have landed you in the bankruptcy court. Her books for the last ten years—I have gone through them carefully—show an expenditure that is positively ruinous. However, I think I have let her see that her housekeeping must be done upon very different lines in future."

"You made her cry very bitterly, poor thing," said his wife. "Her eyes were quite red when she came out of your study."

"Made her cry!" echoed the Captain contemptuously. "She is so fat that the slightest emotion liquefies her. It isn't water, but oil that she sheds when she makes believe to weep."

"She has been a faithful servant to me for the last twenty years," moaned Mrs. Winstanley.

"And she will be a much more faithful servant to you for the next twenty years, if she lives so long. I am not going to send her away. She is an admirable cook, and now she knows that she is not to let your substance run out at the back door, I daresay she will be a fairly good manager. I shall look after her rather sharply, I assure you. I was caterer for our mess three years, and I know pretty well what a household ought to cost per head."

"Oh, Conrad!" cried his wife piteously, "you talk as if we were an institution, or a workhouse, or something horrid."

"My love, a man of sense ought to be able to regulate a private establishment at least as well as a board of thick-headed guardians can regulate a workhouse."

Poor Mrs. Trimmer had left her new master's presence sorely boweddown in spirit. She was so abased that she could only retire to her own snug sitting-room, a panelled parlour, with an ancient ivy-wreathed casement looking into the stable-yard, and indulge herself with what she called "a good cry." It was not until later that she felt equal to communicating her grief to Forbes and Pauline, over the one-o'clock dinner.

She had had a passage of arms, which she denominated "a stand further," with the Captain; but it appeared that her own stand had been feeble. He had been going over the housekeeping accounts for the last ten years—accounts which neither the Squire nor his wife had ever taken the trouble to examine—accounts honestly, but somewhat carelessly and unskillfully made out. There had been an expenditure that was positively scandalous, Captain Winstanley told Mrs. Trimmer.

"If you're dissatisfied, sir, perhaps I'd better go," the old woman said, tremulous with indignation. "If you think there's anything dishonest in my accounts, I wouldn't sleep under this roof another night, though it's been my home near upon forty year—I was kitchen-maid in old Squire Tempest's time —no, I wouldn't stay another hour—not to be doubted."

"I have not questioned your honesty, Trimmer. The accounts are honest enough, I have no doubt, but they show a most unjustifiable waste of money."

"If there's dissatisfaction in your mind, sir, we'd better part. It's always best for both parties. I'm ready to go at an hour's notice, or to stay my month, if it's more convenient to my mistress."

"You are a silly old woman," said the Captain. "I don't want you to go. I am not dissatisfied with you, but with the whole system of housekeeping. There has been a great deal too much given away."

"Not a loaf of bread without my mistress's knowledge," cried Trimmer. "I always told Mrs. Tempest every morning who'd been for soup, or wine, or bread—yes, even to broken victuals—the day before. I had her leave and license for all I did. 'I'm not strong enough to see to the poor things myself, Trimmer,' she used to say, 'but I want them cared for. I leave it all to you.'"

"Very well, Trimmer. That kind of thing must cease from this very hour. Your mistress will contribute to all the local charities. She will give the Vicar an allowance of wine to be distributed by him in urgent cases; but this house will no longer be the village larder—no one is to come to this kitchen for anything.

"What, sir?—not in case of sickness?"

"No. Poor people are always sick. It is their normal state, when there is anything to be got by sickness. There are hospitals and infirmaries for such cases. My house is not to be an infirmary. Do you understand?"

"Yes, sir; I understand that everything is to be different from what it was in my late master's time."

"Precisely. Expenses are to be kept within a certain limit. They are not to fluctuate, as they do in these books of yours. You must get rid of two or three women-servants. There are at least three too many. I am always seeing strange faces about upstairs. One might as well live in a hotel. Think it over, Trimmer, and make up your mind as to which you can best spare, and give them a month's wages, and pack them off. I don't care to have servants about me who are under notice to quit. They always look sulky."

"Is that all, sir?" inquired the housekeeper, drying her angry tears upon her linen apron.

"Well, yes, that is all at present. Stay. What wages has my wife given you?"

"Sixty pounds a year," replied Trimmer, quite prepared to be told that her stipend was to be reduced.

"Then I shall give you seventy."

At this unexpected grace Trimmer began to tremble with an excess of indignation. She saw in this bounty a bribe to meanness.

"Thank you, sir; but I have never asked to have my wages raised, and I am quite contented to remain as I am," she answered with dignity. "Perhaps, if the ways of the house are to be so much altered, I may not feel myself comfortable enough to stay."

"Oh, very well, my good soul; please yourself," replied the Captain carelessly; "but remember what I have told you about cadgers and interlopers; and get rid of two or three of those idle young women. I shall examine your housekeeping accounts weekly, and pay all the tradespeople weekly."

"They have not been used to it, sir."

"Then they must get used to it. I shall pay every account weekly—corn-merchant, and all of them. Bring me up your book on Saturday morning at ten, and let me have all other accounts at the same time."

Here was a revolution. Trimmer and Forbes and Pauline sat long over their dinner, talking about the shipwreck of a fine old house.

"I knew that things would be different," said Pauline, "but I didn't think it would be so bad as this. I thought it would be all the other way, and that there'd be grand doings and lots of company. What awful meanness! Not a drop of soup to be given to a poor family; and I suppose, if I ask my aunt and uncle to stop to tea and supper, anywhen that they call to ask how I am, it will be against the rules."

"From what I gather, there's not a bit nor a sup to be given to mortal," said Mrs. Trimmer solemnly.

"Well, thank Providence, I can afford to buy a bit of tea and sugar and a quart loaf when a friend drops in," said Pauline, "but the meanness isn't any less disgusting. He'll want her to sell her cast-off dresses to the secondhand dealers, I shouldn't wonder."

"And he'll be asking for the keys of the cellars, perhaps," said Forbes, "after I've kept them for five-and-twenty years."

CHAPTER IX.

The Owner of Bullfinch.

Captain Winstanley had been master of the Abbey House three months, and there had been no open quarrel between him and Violet Tempest. Vixen had been cold as marble, but she had been civil. For her mother's sake she had held her peace. She remembered what Roderick Vawdrey had said about her duty, and had tried to do it, difficult as that duty was to the girl's undisciplined nature. She had even taken the loss of Titmouse very quietly— her father's first gift, the pony that had carried her when she was a seven-year-old huntress with tawny hair flowing loose under her little velvet *toque*. She gave no expression to her indignation at the sale of this old favourite, as she had done in the case of Bullfinch. If she wept for him, her tears were shed in secret. She took the sale of her pet almost as a matter of course.

"The Captain thinks we have too many horses and ponies, dear; and you know dear papa was a little extravagant about his stables," said her mother apologetically, when she announced the fate of Titmouse; "but of course Arion will always be kept for you."

"I am glad of that, mamma," Vixen answered gravely. "I should be sorry to part with the last horse papa gave me as well as with the first."

To the Captain himself Vixen said no word about her pony, and he made no apology for or explanation of his conduct, He acted as if Heaven had made him lord of the Abbey House and all its belongings in his cradle, and as if his wife and her daughter were accidental and subordinate figures in the scene of his life.

Despite the era of retrenchment which the new master had inaugurated, things at the Abbey House had never been done with so much dignity and good style. There had been a slipshod ease, an old-fashioned liberality in the housekeeping during the Squire's reign, which had in some measure approximated to the popular idea of an Irish household. Now all was done by line and rule, and according to the latest standard of perfection. There was no new fashion in Belgravia—from a brand of champagne to the shape of a menu-holder—which Captain Winstanley had not at his finger's ends. The old-style expensive heavy dinners at the Abbey House: the monster salmon under whose weight the serving man staggered; the sprawling gigantic turbot, arabesqued with sliced lemon and barberries; the prize turkey, too big for anything but a poultry show; these leviathans and megatheria of the market were seen no more. In their stead came the subdued grace of the *dîner à la Russe*, a well-chosen menu, before composing which Captain Winstanley studied Gouffé's artistic cookery-book as carefully as a pious Israelite studies the Talmud. The new style was as much more economical than the old as it was more elegant. The table, with the Squire's old silver, and fine dark blue and gold Worcester china, and the Captain's picturesque grouping of hothouse flowers and ferns, was a study worthy of a painter of still life. People exclaimed at the beauty of the picture. The grave old dining-room was transformed from its heavy splendour to a modern grace that delighted everybody. Mrs. Winstanley's bosom thrilled with a gentle pride as she sat opposite her husband—he and she facing each other across the centre of the oval table—at their first dinner-party.

"My love, I am delighted that you are pleased," he said afterwards, when she praised his arrangements. "I think I shall be able to show you that economy does not always mean shabbiness. Our dinners shall not be too frequent, but they shall be perfect after their kind."

The Captain made another innovation in his wife's mode of existence. Instead of a daily dropping in of her acquaintance for tea and gossip, she was to have her afternoon, like Lady Ellangowan. A neat copper-plate inscription on her visiting-card told her friends that she was at home on Tuesdays from three to six, and implied that she was not at home on any other day. Mrs. Winstanley felt her dignity enhanced by this arrangement, and the Captain hoped thereby to put a stop to a good deal of twaddling talk, and to lessen the consumption of five-shilling tea, pound-cake, and cream.

The Duke and Duchess returned to Ashbourne with Lady Mabel a short time before Christmas, and the Duchess and her daughter came to one of Mrs. Winstanley's Tuesday afternoons, attended by Roderick Vawdrey. They came with an evident intention of being friendly, and the Duchess was charmed with the old oak hall, the wide hearth and Christmas fire of beech-logs, the light flashing upon the men in armour, and reflected here and there on the beeswaxed panels as on dark water. In this wintry dusk the hall looked its best, dim gleams of colour from the old painted glass mixing with the changeful glow of the fire.

"It reminds me a little of our place in Scotland," said the Duchess, "only this is prettier. It has a warmer homelier air. All things in Scotland have an all-pervading stoniness. It is a country overgrown with granite."

Mrs. Winstanley was delighted to be told that her house resembled one of the ducal abodes.

"I daresay your Scotch castle is much older than this," she said deprecatingly. "We only date from Henry the Eighth. There was an abbey, built in the time of Henry the First; but I am afraid there is nothing left of that but the archway leading into the stables."

"Oh, we are dreadfully ancient at Dundromond; almost as old as the mountains, I should think," answered the Duchess. "Our walls are ten feet thick, and we have an avenue of yew trees said to be a thousand years old. But all that does not prevent the Duke getting bronchitis every time he goes there."

Vixen was in attendance upon her mother, dressed in dark green cloth. Very much the same kind of gown she had on that day at the kennels, Rorie thought, remembering how she looked as she stood with quickened breath and tumbled hair, encircled by those eager boisterous hounds.

"If Landseer could have lived to paint her, I would have given a small fortune for the picture," he thought regretfully.

Lady Mabel was particularly gracious to Violet. She talked about dogs and horses even, in her desire to let herself down to Miss Tempest's level; praised the Forest; made a tentative remark about point lace; and asked Violet if she was fond of Chopin.

"I'm afraid I'm not enlightened enough to care so much for him as I ought." Vixen answered frankly.

"Really! Who is your favourite composer?"

Violet felt as if she were seated before one of those awful books which some young ladies keep instead of albums, in which the sorely-tormented contributor is catechised as to his or her particular tastes, distastes, and failings.

"I think I like Mozart best."

"Do you, really?" inquired Lady Mabel, looking as if Violet had sunk fathoms lower in her estimation by this avowal. "Don't you think that he is dreadfully tuney?"

"I like tunes," retorted Vixen, determined not to be put down. "I'd rather have written '*Voi che sapete*,' and '*Batti, batti*,' than all Chopin's nocturnes and mazurkas."

"I think you would hardly say that if you knew Chopin better," said Lady Mabel gravely, as if she had been gently reproving some one for the utterance of infidel opinions. "When are you coming to see our orchids?" she asked graciously. "Mamma is at home on Thursdays. I hope you and Mrs. Winstanley will drive over and look at my new orchid-house. Papa had it built for me with all the latest improvements. I'm sure you must be fond of orchids, even if you don't appreciate Chopin."

Violet blushed. Rorie was looking on with a malicious grin. He was sitting a little way off in a low Glastonbury chair, with his knees up to his chin, making himself an image of awkwardness.

"I don't believe Violet cares twopence for the best orchid you could show her," he said. "I don't believe your *Dendrobium Formosum* would have any more effect upon her than it has upon me."

"Oh, but I do admire them; or, at least, I should admire them immensely," remonstrated Vixen, "if I could see them in their native country. But I don't know that I have ever thoroughly appreciated them in a hothouse, hanging from the roof, and tumbling on to one's nose, or shooting off their long sprays at a tangent into awkward corners. I'm afraid I like the bluebells and foxgloves in our enclosures ever so much better. I have seen the banks in New Park one sheet of vivid blue with hyacinths, one blaze of crimson with foxgloves; and then there are the long green swamps, where millions of marsh marigolds shine like pools of liquid gold. If I could see orchids blooming like that I should be charmed with them."

"You paint of course," said Lady Mabel. "Wild flowers make delightful studies, do they not?"

Vixen blushed violently.

"I can't paint a little bit," she said. "I am a dreadfully unaccomplished person."

"That's not true," remonstrated Rorie. "She sketches capitally in pen and ink—dogs, horses, trees, you and me, everything, dashed off with no end of spirit."

Here the Duchess, who had been describing the most conspicuous costumes at the German baths, to the delight of Mrs. Winstanley, rose to go, and Lady Mabel, with her graceful, well-drilled air, rose immediately.

"We shall be so glad to see you at Ashbourne," she murmured sweetly, giving Violet her slim little hand in its pearl-gray glove.

She was dressed from head to foot in artistically blended shades of gray—a most unpretending toilet. But to Violet's mind the very modesty of her attire seemed to say: "I am a duke's only daughter, but I don't want to crush you."

Vixen acknowledged her graciousness politely, but without any warmth; and it would hardly have done for Lady Mabel to have known what Miss Tempest said to herself when the Dovedale barouche had driven round the curve of the shrubbery, with Roderick smiling at her from his place as it vanished.

"I am afraid I have a wicked tendency to detest people," said Vixen inwardly. "I feel almost as bad about Lady Mabel as I do about Captain Winstanley."

"Are they not nice?" asked Mrs. Winstanley gushingly, when she and Violet were alone.

"Trimmer's drop-cakes?" said Vixen, who was standing by the tea-table munching a dainty little biscuit. "Yes, they are always capital."

"Nonsense, Violet; I mean the Duchess and her daughter."

Vixen yawned audibly.

"I'm glad you do not find the Duchess insupportably dreary," she said. "Lady Mabel weighed me down like a nightmare."

"Oh Violet! when she behaved so sweetly—quite caressingly, I thought. You really ought to cultivate her friendship. It would be so nice for you to visit at Ashbourne. You would have such opportunities——"

"Of doing what, mamma? Heading polonaises and mazurkas in seven double flats; or seeing orchids with names as long as a German compound adjective."

"Opportunities of being seen and admired by young men of position, Violet. Sooner or later the time must come for you to think of marrying."

"That time will never come, mamma. I shall stay at home with you till you are tired of me, and when you turn me out I will have a cottage in the heart of the Forest—upon some wild ridge topped with a hat of firs—and good old McCroke to take care of me; and I will spend my days botanising and fern-hunting, riding and walking, and perhaps learn to paint my favourite trees, and live as happily and as remote from mankind as the herons in their nests at the top of the tall beeches on Vinny Ridge."

"I am very glad there is no one present to hear you talk like that, Violet," Mrs. Winstanley said gravely.

"Why, mamma?'

"Because anybody hearing you might suppose you were not quite right in your mind."

The Duchess's visit put Mrs. Winstanley in good-humour with all the world, but especially with Roderick Vawdrey. She sent him an invitation to her next dinner, and when her husband seemed inclined to strike his name out of her list, she defended her right of selection with a courage that was almost heroic.

"I can't understand your motive for asking this fellow," the Captain said, with a blacker look than his wife had ever before seen on his countenance.

"Why should I not ask him, Conrad? I have known him ever since he was at Eton, and the dear Squire was very fond of him."

"If you are going to choose your acquaintance in accordance with the taste of your first husband, it will be rather a bad look out for your second," said the Captain.

"What objection can you have to Roderick?"

"I can have, and I have, a very strong objection to him. But I am not going to talk about it yet awhile."

"But, Conrad, if there is anything I ought to know——" began Mrs. Winstanley, alarmed.

"When I think you ought to know it you will be told, my dear Pamela. In the meantime, allow me to have my own opinion about Mr. Vawdrey."

"But, Conrad, in dear Edward's time he used to come to this house whenever he liked, as if he had been a near relation. And he is the Duchess's nephew, remember; and when he marries Lady Mabel, and the Duke dies, he will be one of the largest landowners in South Hampshire."

"Very well, let him come to your dinner. It can make very little difference."

"Now you are offended, Conrad," said Mrs. Winstanley, with a deprecating air.

"No, I am not offended; but I have my own opinion as to your wisdom in giving any encouragement to Mr. Vawdrey."

This sounded mysterious, and made Mrs. Winstanley uncomfortable. But she was determined not to offend the Duchess, who had been so particularly gracious, and who had sent Captain and Mrs. Winstanley a card for a dinner to be given on the last day of the year.

So Roderick got his invitation, and accepted it with friendly promptitude. He was master of the hounds now, and a good many of his days were given up to the pleasures of the hunting-field. He was an important person in his way, full of business; but he generally found time to drop in for an hour on Mrs. Winstanley's Tuesday afternoons, to lounge with his back against the massive oaken chimney-breast and talk to Violet, or pat Argus, while the lady-visitors gossiped and tittered over their tea-cups.

This last dinner of Mrs. Winstanley was to take place a few days before Christmas, and was to be given in honour of a guest who was coming to spend the holidays at the Abbey House. The guest was Captain Winstanley's Irish friend, Lord Mallow, the owner of Bullfinch.

Vixen's heart gave an indignant bound when she heard that he was coming.

"Another person for me to hate," she said to herself, almost despairingly. "I am becoming a mass of envy, hatred, and malice, and all uncharitableness."

Lord Mallow had spent the early morning of life in the army, it appeared, with no particular expectations. He and Captain Winstanley had been brother-officers. But the fell sergeant Death had promoted Patrick Hay to his elder brother's heritage, and he had surrendered a subaltern's place in a line regiment to become Viscount Mallow, and the owner of a fine stretch of fertile hill and valley in County Cork. He had set up at once as the model landlord, eager for his tenantry's welfare, full of advanced ideas, a violent politician, liberal to the verge of radicalism. If the Irish Church had not been disestablished before Lord Mallow went into Parliament, he would have gripped his destructive axe and had a chop or two at the root of that fine old tree. Protestant, and loyal to the Church of England in his own person—so far as such loyalty may be testified by regular attendance at divine service every Sunday morning, and a gentlemanlike reverence for bishops—it seemed to him not the less an injustice that his native land should be taxed with the maintenance of an alien clergy.

The late Lord Mallow had been a violent Tory, Orange to the marrow of his bones. The new Lord Mallow was violently progressive, enthusiastic in his belief in Hibernian virtues, and his indignation at Hibernian wrongs. He wanted to disestablish everything. He saw his country as she appears in the eyes of her poets and song-writers—a fair dishevelled female, oppressed by the cruel Sassenach, a lovely sufferer for whose rescue all true men and leal would fight to the death. He quoted the outrages of Elizabeth's reign, the cruelties of Cromwell's soldiery, the savagery of Ginkell, as if those wrongs had been inflicted yesterday, and the House of Commons of to-day were answerable for them. He made fiery speeches which were reported at length in the Irish newspapers. He was a fine speaker, after a florid pattern, and had a great command of voice, and a certain rugged eloquence that carried his hearers along with him, even when he was harping upon so hackneyed a string as the wrongs of "Ould Ireland."

Lord Mallow was not thirty, and he looked younger than his years. He was tall and broad-shouldered, robust, and a trifle clumsy in figure, and rode fourteen stone. He had a good-looking Irish face, smiling blue eyes, black hair, white teeth, bushy whiskers, and a complexion inclining to rosiness.

"He is the perfection of a commonplace young man," Vixen said, when she talked him over with her mother on the day of his arrival at the Abbey House.

"Come, Violet, you must admit that he is very handsome," remonstrated Mrs. Winstanley, who was sitting before her dressing-room fire, with her feet on a fender-stool of her own crewel-work, waiting for Pauline to commence the important ceremony of dressing for dinner. "I think I never saw a finer set of teeth, and of course at his age they must all be real."

"Unless he has had a few of the original ones knocked out in the hunting-field, mamma. They go over a good many stone walls in Ireland, you know, and he may have come to grief."

"If you would only leave off talking in that horrid way, Violet. He is a very agreeable young man. How he enjoyed a cup of tea after his journey, instead of wanting soda-water and brandy. Conrad tells me he has a lovely place near Mallow—on the slope of a hill, sheltered on the north with pine woods; and I believe it is one of the prettiest parts of Ireland—so green, and fertile, and sweet, and such a happy peasantry."

"I think I'd better leave you to dress for dinner, mamma. You like a clear hour, and it's nearly half-past six."

"True, love; you may ring for Pauline. I have been wavering between my black and maize and my amethyst velvet, but I think I shall decide upon the velvet. What are you going to wear?"

"I? oh, anything. The dress I wore last night."

"My love, it is positively dowdy. Pray wear something better in honour of Lord Mallow. There is the gown you had for my wedding," suggested Mrs. Winstanley, blushing. "You look lovely in that."

"Mamma, do you think I'm going to make a secondhand bridesmaid of myself to oblige Lord Mallow? No; that dress too painfully bears the stamp of what it was made for. I'm afraid it will have to rot in the wardrobe where it hangs. If it were woolen, the moths would inevitably have it; but, I suppose, as it is silk it will survive the changes of time; and some day it will be made into chair-covers, and future generations of Tempests will point to it as a relic of my great-aunt Violet."

"I never heard anything so absurd," cried Mrs. Winstanley fretfully. "It was Theodore's *chef-d'oeuvre*, and no doubt I shall have to pay an awful price for it."

"Ah, mamma, we are continually doing things for which we have to pay an awful price," said Vixen, with one of her involuntary bursts of bitter sadness.

CHAPTER X.

Something like a Ride.

It was impossible to go on hating Lord Mallow for ever. He was a man whose overflowing good-nature would have conciliated the direst foe, could that enemy have been exposed long enough to its softening influence. He came upon the dull daily life of the Abbey House like a burst of sudden sunshine on a gloomy plain. The long winter evenings, when there was no company, had been sorely oppressive to Vixen. Out of respect to her mother she had kept her place in the drawing-room, reading, or working at some uninteresting strip of point-lace, which she had no hope of ever finishing, though it had been promised to Mr. Scobel for his church. Captain Winstanley read the newspapers or the quarterlies, and paced the room thoughtfully at intervals. He talked to his wife just enough to escape the charge of neglect, but rarely spoke to or noticed Violet. Sometimes Mrs. Winstanley asked for a little music; whereupon Violet went to the piano and played her scanty recollections of Mozart or Beethoven—all "tuney" bits, remembered out of the sonatas or symphonies Miss McCroke had taught her; or, if asked to sing, the girl sang a ballad or two, to order, in her full round mezzo-soprano, which had a thrilling expression at times, when feeling got the better of her proud reserve, and all the pent-up sorrow of her heart broke loose into her song. But Captain Winstanley took no notice of these efforts, and even her mother's praises were not enthusiastic.

"Very sweet, very nice," was the most Vixen ever heard from those maternal lips as she closed the piano.

But here was Lord Mallow, passionately fond of music and singing, and the beauties of nature, and all things that appeal to the sensitive Hibernian character. It seemed a new thing to Violet to have someone standing by the piano, turning over the leaves, applauding rapturously, and entreating for another and yet another Irish melody. When she sang "The Minstrel Boy," he joined in with a rich baritone that harmonised finely with her full ripe notes. The old room vibrated with the strong gush of melody, and even Captain Winstanley was impelled to praise.

"How well your voices harmonise," he said. "You ought to try some duets. I remember that fine baritone of yours in days of old, Mallow."

Thereupon Lord Mallow asked Miss Tempest if she had any duets, and Vixen produced her small stock of vocal music. They tried one or two of Mendelssohn's, "I would that my love," and "Greeting," and discovered that they got on wonderfully well together. Vixen fell asleep that night wondering at her own amiability.

"To think that I should sing sentimental duets with him," she said to herself. "The man who has Bullfinch!"

Lord Mallow's presence at the Abbey House had a marked effect upon Captain Winstanley's treatment of his stepdaughter. Hitherto there had been a veiled bitterness in all his speeches, a constrained civility in his manners. Now he was all kindness, all expansion. Even his wife, who admired him always, and thought him the soul of wisdom in all he did, could not be blind to the change, and a new sense of peacefulness stole into her feeble mind. It was so pleasant to see dear Conrad so sweetly kind to Violet.

"What are we going to do with Lord Mallow this morning, Violet?" asked the Captain at breakfast, the day after the Irishman's arrival. "We must try to amuse him somehow."

"I don't think I have much to do with it," Vixen answered coldly. "You will find plenty of amusement, I daresay, in the billiard-room, in the stables, or in showing Lord Mallow your improvements."

"That would do very well for a wet morning, but it would be a profligate waste of fine weather. No; I propose that you should show Mallow some of the prettiest bits in the Forest. I am not half so accomplished a guide as you; but we'll all go. I'll order the horses at once if you like my plan, Mallow," said Captain Winstanley, turning to his friend, and taking Violet's consent for granted.

"I shall be quite too delighted, if Miss Tempest will honour us with her company," replied the Irishman, with a pleasant look at Vixen's fresh morning face, rosy-red with vexation.

It was the first time her stepfather had ever asked her to ride with him, and she hated doing it. It was the first time she had ever been asked to ride with anyone but her father or Roderick Vawdrey. Yet to refuse would have been impossible, without absolute discourtesy to her mother's husband and her mother's guest. So she sat in her place and said nothing; and Lord Mallow mistook the angry carnation for the warm red of happy girlhood, which blushes it knows not wherefore.

Captain Winstanley ordered the horses to be at the door in half-an-hour: and then he took Lord Mallow off to look at the stables, while Violet went upstairs to put on her habit. Why was the Captain so unusually amiable? she speculated. Was his little soul so mean that he put on better manners to do honour to an Irish peer?

She came tripping down the wide old staircase at the end of the half-hour, in habit and hat of Lincoln green, with a cock's feather in the neat little hat, and a formidable hooked hunting-crop for opening gates, little feet daintily shod in patent leather, but no spur. She loved her horse too well to run a needle into his sleek hide at the slightest provocation.

There were three horses, held by Bates and Lord Mallow's groom. Bullfinch, looking as if he had just taken a prize at Islington and was inclined to be bumptious about it. Arion, tossing his delicately modelled Greek head, and peering furtively after bogies in the adjacent shrubbery. Captain Winstanley's well-seasoned hunter, Mosstrooper, nodding his long bony head, and swaying his fine-drawn neck up and down in a half-savage half-scornful manner, as if he were at war with society in general, like the Miller of Dee.

Vixen, who had looked the picture of vexation at the breakfast-table, was now all gaiety. Her hazel eyes sparkled with mischief. Lord Mallow stood in the porch, watching her as she came down the shining oak staircase, glorious in the winter sunlight. He thought her the perfection of a woman—nay, more than a woman, a goddess. Diana, the divine huntress, must have looked so, he fancied. He ran forward to mount her on the fidgety Arion; but honest old Bates was too quick for him; and she was looking down at Lord Mallow graciously from her perch on the well-worn doeskin saddle before he had time to offer his services.

She leaned over to pat Bullfinch's massive crest.

"Dear old horse," she murmured tenderly, remembering those winter mornings of old when he had stood before the porch as he stood to-day, waiting for the noble rider who was never more to mount him.

"Yet life goes on somehow without our beloved dead," thought Violet.

Her changeful face saddened at the idea, and she rode along the shrubberied drive in silence.

"Where are you going to take us?" asked the Captain, when they had emerged from the Abbey House grounds, crossed the coach-road, and made their plunge into the first cart-track that offered itself.

"Everywhere," answered Vixen, with a mischievous laugh. "You have chosen me for your guide, and all you have to do is to follow."

And she gave Arion a light touch with her hunting-crop, and cantered gaily down the gently sloping track to a green lawn, which looked, to Captain Winstanley's experienced eye, very much like a quaggy bog.

"Steer towards your left!" he cried anxiously to Lord Mallow.

If there was danger near Vixen managed to avoid it; she made a sweeping curve, skirted the treacherous-looking lawn, and disappeared in another cart-track, between silvery trunks of veteran beeches, self-sown in the dark ages, with here and there a gnarled old oak, rugged and lichen-mantled, with feathery tufts of fern nestling in the hollow places between his gaunt limbs.

That was a ride! Lord Mallow could remember nothing like it, and he was destined to carry this in his memory for a lifetime. The ghostly trees; the silver-shining bark of the beeches, varying with a hundred indescribable shades of green, and purple, and warmest umber; the rugged gray of the grand old oaks; the lichens and mosses, the mysterious wintry growths of toadstool and weed and berry; that awful air of unearthliness which pervaded the thicker portions of the wood, as of some mystic underworld—half shadow and half dream. No, Lord Mallow could never forget it; nor yet the way that flying figure in Lincoln green led them by bog and swamp, over clay and gravel—through as many varieties of soil as if she had been trying to give them a practical lesson in geology; across snaky ditches and pebbly fords; through furze-bushes and thickets of holly; through everything likely to prove aggravating to the temper of a wellbred horse; and finally, before giving them breathing-time, she led them up the clayey side of a hill, as steep as a house, on the top of which she drew rein, and commanded them to admire the view.

"This is Acres Down, and there are the Needles," she said, pointing her whip at the dim blue horizon. "If it were a clear day, and your sight were long enough, I daresay you would see Jersey, Guernsey, Alderney, and Sark. But, I think, to-day you must be content with the Needles. Can you see them?" she asked Lord Mallow.

"See them!" exclaimed the Irishman. "I can see well enough to thread one of them if I wanted."

"Now, you've seen the Isle of Wight," said Vixen. "That's a point accomplished. The ardent desire of everyone in the Forest is to see the Isle of Wight. They are continually mounting hills and gazing into space, in order to get a glimpse at that chalky little island. It seems the main object of everybody's existence."

"They might as well go and live there at once, if they're so fond of it," suggested Lord Mallon.

"Yes; and then they would be straining their eyes in the endeavour to see the Great Horse—that's a group of firs on the top of a hill, and one of our Forest seamarks. That frantic desire to behold distant objects has always seemed to me to be one of the feeblest tendencies of the human mind. Now you have seen the Needles, we have accomplished a solemn duty, and I may show you our woods."

Vixen shook her rein and trotted recklessly down a slippery path, jumped a broad black ditch, and plunged into the recesses of the wood, Bullfinch and Mosstrooper following meekly.

They went a wonderful round, winding in and out of Bratley Wood, piercing deep into the wintry glories of Mark Ash; through mud and moss and soft pitfalls, where the horses sank up to their hocks in withered leaves; avoiding bogs by a margin of a yard or so; up and down, under spreading branches, where the cattle line but just cleared the heads of the riders; across the blackened bracken; by shining hollies, whose silvery trunks stood up like obelisks out of a thicket of dwarf bushes: through groves, where the tall beech-trunks had a solemn look like the columns of some gigantic temple; then into wondrous plantations of Scotch firs, where the air was balmy as in summer, and no breath of the December wind penetrated the dense wall of foliage. Then to higher ground, where the wintry air blew keen again, and where there was a soft green lawn, studded with graceful conifers—cypress, deodora, Douglas fir—tall with a growth of thirty years; the elegant importations of an advanced civilisation. Anon by the gray lichened walls of a deserted garden, which had a strangely-romantic look, and was as suggestive of a dreamy idyllic world as a poem by Tennyson; and so down into the green-and-gray depths of Mark Ash again, but never returning over the same ground; and then up the hill to Vinny Ridge and the Heronry, where Captain Winstanley cracked his whip to scare the herons, and had the satisfaction of scaring his own and the other two horses, while the herons laughed him to scorn from their cradles in the tree-tops, and would not stir a feather for his gratification. Then by a long plantation to a wild stretch of common, where Vixen told her companions that they were safe for a good while, and set them an example by starting Arion across the short smooth turf at a hand-gallop. They pulled up just in time to escape a small gulf of moss and general sponginess, waded a stream or two, splashed through a good deal of spewy ground, and came to Queen's Bower; thence into the oak plantations of New Park; then across Gretnam Wood; and then at a smart trot along the road towards home.

"I hope I haven't kept you out too long?" said Vixen politely.

"We've only been five hours," answered the Captain with grim civility; "but if Mallow is not tired, I shall not complain."

"I never enjoyed anything so much in my life, never," protested Lord Mallow.

"Well, to-morrow we can shoot the pheasants. It will be a rest for us after this."

"It will be dull work after the enchantments of to-day," said the Irishman.

Captain Winstanley rode homewards a few paces in the rear of the other two, smiling to himself grimly, and humming a little song of Heine's:

"Es ist eine alte Geschichte,
Doch bleibt sie immer neu."

CHAPTER XI.

Rorie objects to Duets.

Mrs. Winstanley's little dinner went off smoothly and pleasantly, as all such entertainments had done under the new *régime*. The Captain knew how to select his guests, as well as he knew how to compose a *menu*. People felt pleased with themselves and with their neighbours at his table. There was nothing heavy in the dinner or in the conversation; there were no long sittings over old port or particular claret. The wines were of the first quality; but there was no fuss made about them. Colonel Carteret remembered how he and the Squire had sat prosing over their port or Château Lafitte, and felt as if he were living in a new world—a world in which full-blooded friendship and boisterous hospitality were out of fashion. People whose talk had hitherto been intensely local—confined, for the most part to petty sessions, commoners' rights, hunting, and the parish church and schools—found themselves discussing the widest range of topics, from the prospect of a European war—that European war which has been impending more or less distinctly for the last twenty years—to the latest social scandal in the upper currents of London society. Captain and Mrs. Winstanley's country friends, inspired by one or two clever young men just imported from the London clubs, were surprised to discover how well they were able to criticise the latest productions in literature, art, and the drama; the newest results of scientific investigation; or the last record of African or Central Asian exploration. It was quite delightful to quiet country people, who went to London on an average once in three years, to find themselves talking so easily about the last famous picture, the latest action for libel in artistic circles, or the promised adaptation of Sardou's last comedy at a West End theatre, just as glibly as if they knew all about art, and had read every play of Sardou's.

Roderick Vawdrey enjoyed himself wonderfully at this particular dinner-party, so long as the dinner lasted; for Captain Winstanley, by an oversight which made him inwardly savage all dinner-time, had placed Mr. Vawdrey and Miss Tempest side by side. There had been some confusion in his mind as he finished his plan of the table; his attention having been called away at the last moment, or this thing could not have happened—for nothing was farther from Captain Winstanley's intention than that Violet and her old playfellow should be happy in each other's society. And there they sat, smiling and sparkling at each other in the exuberance of youth and high spirits, interchanging little confidential remarks that were doubtless to the disparagement of some person or persons in the assembly. If dark electric glances shot from the covert of bent brows could have slain those two happy triflers, assuredly neither of them would have lived to the end of that dinner.

"How do you like him?" asked Rorie, stooping to sniff at the big Maréchal Niel bud, in the specimen glass by his plate.

"Whom?"

"The man who has Bullfinch."

Lord Mallow was in the place of honour next his hostess. Involuntarily Violet glanced in that direction, and was startled to find the Irishman's good-humoured gaze meeting hers, just as if he had been watching her for the last half-hour.

"How do I like him? Well, he seems very good-natured."

"Seems good-natured. You ought to be able to give me a more definite answer by this time. You have lived in the same house with him—let me see, is it three or four days since he came?"

"He has been here nearly a week."

"A week! Why then you must know him as well as if he were your brother. There is no man living who could keep himself dark for a week. No; I don't believe the most inscrutable of men, born and bred in diplomatic circles, could keep the secret of a solitary failing from the eyes of those who live under the same roof with him for seven days. It would leak out somehow—if not at breakfast, at dinner. Man is a communicative animal, and so loves talking of himself that if he has committed murder he must tell somebody about it sooner or later. And as to that man," continued Rorie, with a contemptuous glance at the single-minded Lord Mallow, "he is a creature whom the merest beginner in the study of humanity would know by heart in half-an-hour."

"What do you know about him?" asked Vixen laughing. "You have had more than half-an-hour for the study of his character."

"I know ever so much more than I want to know."

"Answered like a Greek oracle."

"What, have you taken to reading Greek?"

"No; but I know the oracles were a provoking set of creatures who answered every inquiry with an enigma. But I won't have you abuse Lord Mallow. He has been very kind to Bullfinch, and has promised me that he will never part with him. The dear old horse is to have a comfortable stable and kindly treatment to his dying day—not to be sent out to grass in his old age, to shiver in a dreary solitude, or to be scorched by the sun and tormented by the flies."

"He has promised all that, has he? He would promise a good deal more, I daresay," muttered Rorie, stooping over his rosebud. "Do you think him handsome? Do women admire a fresh complexion and black whiskers, and that unmistakable air of a hairdresser's wax model endowed with animation?"

"I see you consider him an idiot," said Vixen laughing. "But I assure you he is rather clever. He talks wonderfully about Ireland, and the reforms he is going to bring about for her."

"Of course. Burke, and Curran, and Castlereagh, and O'Connell, and fifty more have failed to steer that lumbering old vessel off the mudbank on which she stranded at some time in the dark ages; in fact, nobody except Oliver Cromwell ever did understand how to make Ireland prosperous and respectable, and he began by depopulating her. And here is a fresh-coloured young man, with whiskers à la côtelette de mouton, who thinks he was born to be her pilot, and to navigate her into a peaceful haven. He is the sort of man who will begin by being the idol of a happy tenantry, and end by being shot from behind one of his own hedges."

"I hope not," said Vixen, "for I am sure he means well. And I should like him to outlive Bullfinch."

Roderick had been very happy all dinner-time. From the soups to the ice-puddings the moments had flown for him. It seemed the briefest dinner he had ever been at; and yet when the ladies rose to depart the silvery chime of the clock struck the half-hour after nine. But Lord Mallow's hour came later, in the drawing-room, where he contrived to hover over Violet, and fence her round from all other admirers for the rest of the evening. They sang their favourite duets together, to the delight of everyone except Rorie, who felt curiously savage at "I would that my love," and icily disapproving at "Greeting;" but vindictive to the verge of homicidal mania at "Oh, wert thou in the cauld blast!"

"His 'plaidie,' indeed," he ejaculated inwardly. "The creature never possessed anything so comfortable or civilised. How preposterous it is to hear an Irishman sing Scotch songs. If an Irishman had a plaidie, he would pawn it for a dhrop o' the cratur."

Later Violet and Lord Mallow sang a little duet by Masini, "*O, que la mer est belle!*" the daintiest, most bewitching music—such a melody as the Loreley might have sung when the Rhine flowed peacefully onward below mountain-peaks shining in the evening light, luring foolish fishermen to their doom. Everybody was delighted. It was just the kind of music to please the unlearned in the art. Mrs. Carteret came to the piano to compliment Violet.

"I had no idea you could sing so sweetly," she said. "Why have you never sung to us before?"

"Nobody ever asked me," Vixen answered frankly. "But indeed I am no singer."

"You have one of the freshest, brightest voices I ever had the happiness of hearing," Lord Mallow exclaimed enthusiastically.

He would have liked to go on singing duets for an indefinite period. He felt lifted into some strange and delightful region—a sphere of love and harmony—while he was mingling his voice with Violet's. It made the popular idea of heaven, as a place where there is nothing but singing—an eternal, untiring choir—clearer and more possible to him than it had ever seemed before. Paradise would be quite endurable if he and Violet might stand side by side in the serried ranks of choristers. There was quite a little crowd round the piano, shutting in Violet and Lord Hallow, and Roderick Vawdrey was not in it. He felt himself excluded, and held himself gloomily apart, talking hunting talk with a man for whom he did not care twopence. Directly his carriage was announced—*sotto voce* by the considerate Forbes, so as not to wound anybody's feelings by the suggestion that the festivity was on its last legs—Mr. Vawdrey went up to Mrs. Winstanley and took leave. He would not wait to say good-night to Violet. He only cast one glance in the direction of the piano, where the noble breadth of Mrs. Carteret's brocaded amber back obscured every remoter object, and then went away moodily, denouncing duet-singing as an abomination.

When Lady Mabel asked him next day what kind of an evening he had had at the Abbey House, in a tone which implied that any entertainment there must be on a distinctly lower level as compared with the hospitalities of Ashbourne, he told her that it had been uncommonly slow.

"How was that? You had some stupid person to take into dinner, perhaps?"

"No; I went in with Violet."

"And you and she are such old friends. You ought to get on very well together."

Rorie reddened furiously. Happily he was standing with his back to the light in one of the orchid-houses, enjoying the drowsy warmth of the atmosphere, and Mabel was engrossed with the contemplation of a fine zygopetalum, which was just making up its mind to bloom.

"Oh, yes, that was well enough; but the evening was disgustingly slow. There was too much music."

"Classical?"

"Lord knows. It was mostly French and German. I consider it an insult to people to ask them to your house, and then stick them down in their chairs, and say h—sh—h! every time they open their months. If people want to give amateur concerts, let them say so when they send out their invitations, and then one would know what one has to expect."

"I am afraid the music must have been very bad to make you so cross," said Lady Mabel, rather pleased that the evening at the Abbey House should have been a failure. "Who were the performers?"

"Violet, and an Irish friend of Captain Winstanley's—a man with a rosy complexion and black whiskers—Lord Mallow."

"Lord Mallow! I think I danced with him once or twice last season. He is rather distinguished as a politician, I believe, among the young Ireland party. Dreadfully radical."

"He looks it," answered Rorie. "He has a loud voice and a loud laugh, and they seem to be making a great deal of him at the Abbey House."

"'Tommy loves a lord,'" says Lady Mabel brightly. Rorie hadn't the faintest idea whence the quotation came. "I daresay the Winstanleys are rather glad to have Lord Mallow staying with them."

"The Squire would have kicked him out of doors," muttered Rorie savagely.

"But why? Is he so very objectionable? He waltzes beautifully, if I remember right; and I thought him rather a well-meaning young man."

"Oh, there's nothing serious against him that I know of; only I don't think Squire Tempest would have liked a singing man any more than he would have liked a singing mouse."

"I didn't know Miss Tempest sang," said Lady Mabel. "I thought she could do nothing but ride."

"Oh, she has a very pretty voice, but one may have too much of a good thing, you know. One doesn't go out to dinner to hear people sing duets."

"I'm afraid they must have given you a very bad dinner, or you would hardly be so cross. I know that is the way with papa. If the dinner is bad he abuses everything, and declares the ladies were all ugly."

"Oh, the dinner was excellent, I believe. I'm not a connoisseur, like my uncle. People might give me the most wonderful dinner in the world, and I would hardly be the wiser; or they might give me a wretched one, and I should not feel particularly angry with them."

The next day was Tuesday, and, as the Duchess and her daughter happened to be driving within a mile or so of the Abbey House, Lady Mabel suggested that they should call upon Mrs. Winstanley.

"I am rather anxious to see the wild Irishman they have captured lately— Lord Mallow. We met him at Lady Dumdrum's, if you remember, mamma. I danced with him twice."

"My dear Mabel, do you think I can remember all your partners?"

"But Lord Mallow is rather celebrated. He makes very good speeches. Papa read one of them to us the other day when there was a great debate going on upon the Irish land question."

The Duchess remembered being read to one evening after dinner, but the debates, as delivered by the Duke, had generally a somnolent effect upon his wife. She had a faint idea of the beginning, and struggled heroically to discover what the speakers were talking about; then came a soft confusion of sound, like the falling of waters; and the middle and end of the debate was dreamland. Lady Mabel was of a more energetic temper, and was interested in everything that could enlarge her sphere of knowledge, from a parliamentary debate to a Greek play.

The Duchess had never in her life refused compliance with any wish of her daughter's, so the horses' heads were turned towards the Abbey House, along a smooth hard road through a pine wood, then through a lodge-gate into a forest of rhododendrons.

"This is really a nicer place than Ashbourne, mamma," remarked Lady Mabel disapprovingly.

It appeared to her quite a mistake in the arrangement of the universe that Violet Tempest should be heiress to a more picturesque estate than that which she, the Duke of Dovedale's only daughter, was to inherit.

"My dear, Ashbourne is perfect. Everyone says so. The stables, the offices, the way the house is lighted and heated, the ventilation."

"Yes, mamma; but those are details which nobody thinks about except an architect or a house-agent. Ashbourne is so revoltingly modern. It smells of stucco. It will take a century to tone it down. Now this fine old place is like a dream of the past; it is a poem in wood and stone. Ashbourne would be very well for a hunting-box for anyone who had three or four other places, as my father has; but when my time comes, and I have only Ashbourne, I'm afraid I shall hate it."

"But you will have a choice of places by-and-by," said the Duchess consolingly "You will have Briarwood."

"Briarwood is a degree uglier than Ashbourne," sighed Lady Mabel, leaning back in the carriage, wrapped to the chin in Russian sable, the image of discontent.

There are moments in every life, as in Solomon's, when all seems vanity. Lady Mabel Ashbourne's life had been cloudless—a continual summer, an unchangeable Italian sky; and yet there were times when she was weary of it, when some voice within her murmured, "This is not enough." She was pretty, she was graceful, accomplished, gifted with a self-confidence that generally passed for wit; all the blood in her veins was the bluest of the blue, everybody bowed down to her, more or less, and paid her homage; the man she liked best in the world, and had so preferred from her childhood, was to be her husband; nobody had ever contradicted her, or hinted that she was less than perfect; and yet that mysterious and rebellious voice sometimes repeated, "It is not enough." She was like the woman in the German fairy tale, who, beginning as the wife of a half-starved fisherman, came, by fairy power, to be king, and then emperor, and then pope: and still was not contented, but languished for something more, aye, even to have the ordering of the sun and moon.

The rebellious voice expostulated loudly this winter afternoon, as Lady Mabel's languid eyes scanned the dark shining rhododendron bushes, rising bank above bank, a veritable jungle, backed by tall beeches and towerlike Douglas firs. A blackbird was whistling joyously amongst the greenery, and a robin was singing on the other side of the drive. The sunlit sky was soft and pearly. It was one of those mild winters in which Christmas steals unawares upon the footprints of a lovely autumn. The legendary oak was doubtless in full bud at Cadenham, like its miraculous brother, the Glastonbury thorn.

"I don't think any of my father's places can compare with this," Lady Mabel said irritably.

She would not have minded the beauty of the grounds so much had they been the heritage of any other heiress than Violet Tempest.

The old hall was full of people and voices when the Duchess and her daughter were announced. There was a momentary hush at their entrance, as at the advent of someone of importance, and Mrs. Winstanley came smiling out of the firelight to welcome them, in Theodore's last invention, which was a kind of skirt that necessitated a peculiar gliding motion in the wearer, and was built upon the lines of a mermaid's tail.

"How good of you!" exclaimed Mrs. Winstanley.

"We were coming through Lyndhurst, and could not resist the temptation of coming in to see you," said the Duchess graciously. "How do you do, Miss Tempest? Were you out with the hounds this morning? We met some people riding home."

"I have never hunted since my father's death," Violet answered gravely; and the Duchess was charmed with the answer and the seriously tender look that accompanied it.

Lord Mallow was standing before the hearth, looking remarkably handsome in full hunting costume. The well-worn scarlet coat and high black boots became him. He had enjoyed his first day with the Forest hounds, had escaped the bogs, and had avoided making an Absalom of himself among the spreading beechen boughs. Bullfinch had behaved superbly over his old ground.

Mr. and Mrs. Scobel were among those dusky figures grouped around the wide firelit hearth, where the piled-up logs testified to the Tempest common of estovers. Mr. Scobel was talking about the last advance movement of the Ritualists, and expatiating learnedly upon the Ornaments Rubric of 1559, and its bearing upon the Advertisements of 1566, with a great deal more about King Edward's first Prayer-book, and the Act of Uniformity, to Colonel Carteret, who, from an antique conservative standpoint, regarded Ritualists, Spirit-rappers, and Shakers in about the same category; while Mrs. Scobel twittered cheerily about the parish and the schools to the Colonel's bulky wife, who was a liberal patroness of all philanthropic institutions in her neighbourhood.

Lord Mallow came eagerly forward to recall himself to the memories of Lady Mabel and her mother.

"I hope your grace has not forgotten me," he said; and the Duchess, who had not the faintest recollection of his face or figure, knew that this must be Lord Mallow. "I had the honour of being introduced to you at Lady Dumdrum's delightful ball."

The Duchess said something gracious, and left Lord Mallow free to talk to Lady Mabel. He reminded her of that never to be, by him, forgotten waltz, and talked, in his low-pitched Irish voice, as if he had lived upon nothing but the recollection of it ever since.

It was idiosyncratic of Lord Mallow that he could not talk to any young woman without seeming to adore her. At this very moment he thought Violet Tempest the one lovable and soul-entrancing woman the world held for him; yet at sight of Lady Mabel he behaved as if she and no other was his one particular star.

"It was a nice dance, wasn't it? but there were too many people for the rooms," said Lady Mabel easily; "and I don't think the flowers were so prettily arranged as the year before. Do you?"

"I was not there the year before."

"No? I must confess to having been at three balls at Lady Dumdrum's. That makes me seem very old, does it not? Some young ladies in London make believe to be always in their first season. They put on a hoydenish freshness, and pretend to be delighted with everything, as if they were just out of the nursery."

"That's a very good idea up to thirty," said Lord Mallow. "I should think it would hardly answer after."

"Oh, after thirty they begin to be fond of horses and take to betting. I believe young ladies after thirty are the most desperate—what is that dreadful slang word?—plungers in society. How do you like our hunting?"

"I like riding about the Forest amazingly; but I should hardly call it hunting, after Leicestershire. Of course that depends in a measure upon what you mean by hunting. If you only mean hounds pottering about after a fox, this might pass muster; but if your idea of hunting includes hard riding and five-barred gates, I should call the kind of thing you do here by another name."

"Was my cousin, Mr. Vawdrey, out to-day?"

"The M. F. H.? In the first flight. May I get you some tea?"

"If you please. Mrs. Winstanley's tea is always so good."

Mrs. Winstanley was supremely happy in officiating at her gipsy table, where the silver tea-kettle of Queen Anne's time was going through its usual sputtering performances. To sit in a fashionable gown—however difficult the gown might be to sit in—and dispense tea to a local duchess, was Mrs. Winstanley's loftiest idea of earthly happiness. Of course there might be a superior kind of happiness beyond earth; but to appreciate that the weak human soul would have to go through a troublesome ordeal in the way of preparation, as the gray cloth at Hoyle's printing-works is dashed about in gigantic vats, and whirled round upon mighty wheels, before it is ready for the reception of particular patterns and dyes.

Lady Mabel and Lord Mallow had a longish chat in the deep-set window where Vixen watched for Rorie on his twenty-first birthday. The conversation came round to Irish politics somehow, and Lord Mallow was enraptured at discovering that Lady Mabel had read his speeches, or had heard them read. He had met many young ladies who professed to be interested in his Irish politics; but never before had he encountered one who seemed to know what she was talking about. Lord Mallow was enchanted. He had found his host's lively step-daughter stonily indifferent to the Hibernian cause. She had said "Poor things" once or twice, when he dilated on the wrongs of an oppressed people; but her ideas upon all Hibernian subjects were narrow. She seemed to imagine Ireland a vast expanse of bog chiefly inhabited by pigs.

"There are mountains, are there not?" she remarked once; "and tourists go there? But people don't live there, do they?'

"My dear Miss Tempest, there are charming country seats; if you were to see the outskirts of Waterford, or the hills above Cork, you would find almost as many fine mansions as in England."

"Really?" exclaimed Vixen, with most bewitching incredulity; "but people don't live in them? Now I'm sure you cannot tell me honestly that anyone lives in Ireland. You, for instance, you talk most enthusiastically about your beautiful country, but you don't live in it."

"I go there every year for the fishing."

"Yes; but gentlemen will go to the most uncomfortable places for fishing —Norway, for example. You go to Ireland just as you go to Norway."

"I admit that the fishing in Connemara is rather remote from civilisation ____."

"Of course. It is at the other end of everything. And then you go into the House of Commons, and rave about Ireland, just as if you loved her as I love the Forest, where I hope to live and die. I think all this wild enthusiasm about Ireland is the silliest thing in the world when it comes from the lips of landowners who won't pay their beloved country the compliment of six months' residence out of the twelve."

After this Lord Mallow gave up all hope of sympathy from Miss Tempest. What could be expected from a young lady who could not understand patriotism in the abstract, but wanted to pin a man down for life to the spot of ground for which his soul burned with the ardour of an orator and a poet? Imagine Tom Moore compelled to live in a humble cot in the Vale of Avoca! He infinitely preferred his humdrum cottage in Wiltshire. Indeed, I believe it has been proved against him that he had never seen the Meeting of the Waters, and wrote about that famous scene from hearsay. Ireland has never had a poet as Irish as Burns and Scott were Scottish. Her whole-hearted, single-minded national bard has yet to be born.

It was a relief, therefore, to Lord Mallow's active mind to find himself in conversation with a young lady who really cared for his subject and understood him. He could have talked to Lady Mabel for ever. The limits of five-o'clock tea were far too narrow. He was delighted when the Duchess paused as she was going away, and said:

"I hope you will come and see us at Ashbourne, Lord Mallow; the Duke will be very pleased to know you."

Lord Mallow murmured something expressive of a mild ecstasy, and the Duchess swept onward, like an Australian clipper with all sails set, Lady Mabel gliding like a neat little pinnace in her wake.

Lord Mallow was glad when the next day's post brought him a card of invitation to the ducal dinner on December the 31st. He fancied that he was indebted to Lady Mabel for this civility.

"You are going, of course," he said to Violet, twisting the card between his fingers meditatively.

"I believe I am asked."

"She is," answered Mrs. Winstanley, from her seat behind the urn; "and I consider, under the circumstances, it is extremely kind of the Duchess to invite her."

"Why?" asked Lord Mallow, intensely mystified.

"Why, the truth is, my dear Lord Mallow, that Violet is in an anomalous position. She has been to Lady Southminster's ball, and a great many parties about here. She is out and yet not out, if you understand."

Lord Mallow looked as if he was very far from understanding.

"She has never been presented," explained Mrs. Winstanley. "It is too dreadful to think of. People would call me the most neglectful of mothers. But the season before last seemed too soon alter dear Edward's death, and last season, well"—blushing and hesitating a little—"my mind was so much occupied, and Violet herself was so indifferent about it, that somehow or other the time slipped by and the thing was not done. I feel myself awfully to blame —almost as much so as if I had neglected her confirmation. But early next season—at the very first drawing-room, if possible—she must be presented, and then I shall feel a great deal more comfortable in my mind."

"I don't think it matters one little bit," said Lord Mallow, with appalling recklessness.

"It would matter immensely if we were travelling. Violet could not be presented at any foreign court, or invited to any court ball. She would be an outcast. I shall have to be presented myself, on my marriage with Captain Winstanley. We shall go to London early in the spring. Conrad will take a small house in Mayfair."

"If I can get one," said the captain doubtfully. "Small houses in Mayfair are as hard to get nowadays as black pearls—and as dear."

"I am charmed to think you will be in town," exclaimed Lord Mallow; "and, perhaps, some night when there is an Irish question on, you and Miss Tempest might be induced to come to the Ladies' Gallery. Some ladies rather enjoy a spirited debate."

"I should like it amazingly," cried Violet. "You are awfully rude to one another, are you not? And you imitate cocks and hens; and do all manner of dreadful things. It must be capital fun."

This was not at all the kind of appreciation Lord Mallow desired.

"Oh, yes; we are excruciatingly funny sometimes, I daresay, without knowing it," he said, with a mortified air.

He was getting on the friendliest terms with Violet. He was almost as much at home with her as Rorie was, except that she never called him by his christian-name, nor flashed at him those lovely mirth-provoking glances which he surprised sometimes on their way to Mr. Vawdrey. Those two had a hundred small jokes and secrets that dated back to Vixen's childhood. How could a new-comer hope to be on such delightful terms with her? Lord Mallow felt this, and hated Roderick Vawdrey as intensely as it was possible for a nature radically good and generous to hate even a favoured rival. That Roderick was his rival, and was favoured, were two ideas of which Lord Mallow could not dispossess himself, notwithstanding the established fact of Mr. Vawdrey's engagement to his cousin.

"A good many men begin life by being engaged to their cousins," reflected Lord Mallow. "A man's relations take it into their heads to keep an estate in the family, and he is forthwith set at his cousin like an unwilling terrier at a rat. I don't at all feel as if this young man were permanently disposed of, in spite of all their talk; and I'm very sure Miss Tempest likes him better than I should approve of were I the cousin."

While he loitered over his second cup of coffee, with the ducal card of invitation in his hand, it seemed to him a good opportunity for talking about Lady Mabel.

"A very elegant girl, Lady Mabel," he said; "and remarkably clever. I never talked to a young woman, or an old one either, who knew so much about Ireland. She's engaged to that gawky cousin, isn't she?"

Vixen shot an indignant look at him, and pouted her rosy underlip.

"You mean young Vawdrey. Yes; it is quite an old engagement. They were affianced to each other in their cradles, I believe," answered Captain Winstanley.

"Just what I should have imagined," said Lord Mallow.

"Why?"

"Because they seem to care so little for each other now."

"Oh but, dear Lord Mallow, remember Lady Mabel Ashbourne is too well-bred to go about the world advertising her affection for her future husband," remonstrated Mrs. Winstanley. "I'm sure, if you had seen us before our marriage, you would never have guessed from our manner to each other that Conrad and I were engaged. You would not have a lady behave like a housemaid with her 'young man.' I believe in that class of life they always sit with their arms round each other's waists at evening parties."

"I would have a lady show that she has a heart, and is not ashamed to acknowledge its master," said Lord Mallow, with his eyes on Vixen, who sat stolidly silent, pale with anger. "However, we will put down Lady Mabel's seeming coldness to good-breeding. But as to Mr. Vawdrey, all I can say about him is, that he may be in love with his cousin's estate, but he is certainly not in love with his cousin."

This was more than Vixen could brook.

"Mr. Vawdrey is a gentleman, with a fine estate of his own!" she cried. "How dare you impute such meanness to him?"

"It may be mean, but it is the commonest thing in life."

"Yes, among adventurers who have no other road to fortune than by marrying for money; but do you suppose it can matter to Roderick whether he has a thousand acres less or more, or two houses instead of one? He is going to marry Lady Mabel because it was the dearest wish of his mother's heart, and because she is perfect, and proper, and accomplished, and wonderfully clever—you said as much yourself—and exactly the kind of wife that a young man would be proud of. There are reasons enough, I should hope," concluded Vixen indignantly.

She had spoken breathlessly, in gasps of a few words at a time, and her eyes flashed their angriest light upon the astounded Irishman.

"Not half a reason if he does not love her," he answered boldly. "But I believe young Englishmen of the present day marry for reason and not for love. Cupid has been cashiered in favour of Minerva. Foolish marriages are out of fashion. Nobody ever thinks of love in a cottage. First, there are no more cottages; and secondly, there is no more love."

Christmas was close at hand: a trying time for Vixen, who remembered the jolly old Christmas of days gone by, when the poor from all the surrounding villages came to receive the Squire's lavish bounty, and not even the tramp or the cadger was sent empty-handed away. Under the new master all was done by line and rule. The distribution of coals and blankets took place down in Beechdale under Mr. and Mrs. Scobel's management. Vixen went about from cottage to cottage, in the wintry dusk, giving her small offerings out of her scanty allowance of pocket-money, which Captain Winstanley had put at the lowest figure he decently could.

"What can Violet want with pocket-money?" he asked, when he discussed the subject with his wife. "Your dressmaker supplies all her gowns, and bonnets, and hats. You give her gloves—everything. Nobody calls upon her for anything."

"Her papa always gave her a good deal of money," pleaded Mrs. Winstanley. "I think she gave it almost all away to the poor."

"Naturally. She went about pauperising honest people because she had more money than she knew what to do with. Let her have ten pounds a quarter to buy gloves and eau-de-cologne, writing-paper, and postage-stamps, and trifles of that kind. She can't do much harm with that, and it is quite as much as you can afford, since we have both made up our minds to live within our incomes."

Mrs. Winstanley sighed and assented, as she was wont to do. It seemed hard that there should be this need of economy, but it was in a manner Violet's fault that they were all thus restricted, since she was to take so much, and to reduce her mother almost to penury by-and-by.

"I don't know what would become of me without Conrad's care," thought the dutiful wife.

Going among her poor this Christmas, with almost empty hands, Violet Tempest discovered what it was to be really loved. Honest eyes brightened none the less at her coming, the little children flocked as fondly to her knee. The changes at the Abbey House were very well understood. They were all put down to Captain Winstanley's account; and many a simple heart burned with indignation at the idea that the Squire's golden-haired daughter was being "put upon."

One bright afternoon in the Christmas holidays Vixen consented, half reluctantly, to let Lord Mallow accompany her in her visits among the familiar faces. That was a rare day for the Squire's old pensioners. The Irishman's pockets were full of half-crowns and florins and sixpences for the rosy-faced, bare-footed, dirty, happy children.

"It puts me in mind of the old country," he said, when he had made acquaintance with the interior of half-a-dozen cottages. "The people seem just as kind and friendly, and improvident, and idle, and happy-go-lucky as my friends at home. That old Sassenach Forester, now, that we saw sitting in the winter sun, drinking his noon-day pint, on a bench outside a rustic beer-shop, looking the very image of rustic enjoyment—what Irishman could take life more lightly or seem better pleased with himself? a freeborn child of the sun and wind, ready to earn his living anyhow, except by the work of his hands. Yes, Miss Tempest, I feel a national affinity to your children of the Forest. I wish I were Mr. Vawdrey, and bound to spend my life here."

"Why, what would life be to you if you had not Ould Ireland to fight for?" cried Vixen, smiling at him.

"Life would be simply perfect for me if I had——"

"What?" asked Vixen, as he came to a sudden stop.

"The dearest wish of my heart. But I dare not tell you what that is yet awhile."

Vixen felt very sorry she had asked the question. She looked wildly round for another cottage. They had just done the last habitation in a straggling village in the heart of the woods. There was nothing human in sight by which the conversation might be diverted from the uncomfortable turn it had just taken. Yes; yonder under the beechen boughs Vixen descried a small child with red legs, like a Jersey partridge, dragging a smaller child by the arm, ankle-deep in the sodden leaves. To see them, and to dart across the wet grass towards them were almost simultaneous.

"Tommy," cried Vixen, seizing the red-legged child, "why do you never come to the Abbey House?"

"Because Mrs. Trimmer says there's nothing for me," lisped the infant. "The new master sells the milk up in Lunnun."

"Laudable economy," exclaimed Vixen to Lord Mallow, who had followed her into the damp woodland and heard the boy's answer. "The poor old Abbey House can hardly know itself under such admirable management."

"There is as big a house where you might do what you liked; yes, and give away the cows as well as the milk, if you pleased, and none should say you nay," said Lord Mallow in a low voice, full of unaffected tenderness.

"Oh, please don't!" cried Vixen; "don't speak too kindly. I feel sometimes as if one little kind word too much would make me cry like a child. It's the last straw, you know, that crushes the camel; and I hate myself for being so weak and foolish."

After this Vixen walked home as if she had been winning a match, and Lord Mallow, for his life, dared not say another tender word.

This was their last *tête-à-tête* for some time. Christmas came with its festivities, all of a placid and eminently well-bred character, and then came the last day of the year and the dinner at Ashbourne.

CHAPTER XII.

"Fading in Music."

"Mrs. Winstanley, on her marriage, by the Duchess of Dovedale."

That was the sentence that went on repeating itself like a cabalistic formula in Pamela Winstanley's mind, as her carriage drove through the dark silent woods to Ashbourne on the last night of the year.

A small idea had taken possession of her small mind. The Duchess was the fittest person to present her to her gracious mistress, or her gracious mistress's representative, at the first drawing-room of the coming season. Mrs. Winstanley had old friends, friends who had known her in her girlhood, who would have been happy to undertake the office. Captain Winstanley had an ancient female relative, living in a fossil state at Hampton Court, and vaguely spoken of as "a connection," who would willingly emerge from her aristocratic hermitage to present her kinsman's bride to her sovereign, and whom the Captain deemed the proper sponsor for his wife on that solemn occasion. But what social value had a fossilised Lady Susan Winstanley, of whom an outside world knew nothing, when weighed in the balance with the Duchess of Dovedale? No; Mrs. Winstanley felt that to be presented by the Duchess was the one thing needful to her happiness.

It was a dinner of thirty people; quite a state dinner. The finest and newest orchids had been brought out of their houses, and the dinner-table looked like a tropical forest in little. Vixen went in to dinner with Lord Ellangowan, which was an unappreciated honour, as that nobleman had very little to say for himself, except under extreme pressure, and in his normal state could only smile and look good-natured. Roderick Vawdrey was ever so far away, between his betrothed and an enormous dowager in sky-blue velvet and diamonds.

After dinner there was music. Lady Mabel played a dreary minor melody, chiefly remarkable for its delicate modulation from sharps to flats and back again. A large gentleman sang an Italian buffo song, at which the company smiled tepidly; a small young lady sighed and languished through "Non e ver;" and then Miss Tempest and Lord Mallow sang a duet.

This was the success of the evening. They were asked to sing again and again. They were allowed to monopolise the piano; and before the evening was over everyone had decided that Lord Mallow and Miss Tempest were engaged. Only the voices of plighted lovers could be expected to harmonise as well as that.

"They must have sung very often together," said the Duchess to Mrs. Winstanley.

"Only within the last fortnight. Lord Mallow never stayed with us before, you know. He is my husband's friend. They were brother-officers, and have known each other a long time. Lord Mallow insists upon Violet singing every evening. He is passionately fond of music."

"Very pleasant," murmured the Duchess approvingly: and then she glided on to shed the sunshine of her presence upon another group of guests.

Carriages began to be announced at eleven—that is to say, about half-an-hour after the gentlemen had left the dining-room—but the Duke insisted that people should stop till twelve.

"We must see the old year out," he said. "It is a lovely night. We can go out on the terrace and hear the Ringwood bells."

This is how Violet and Lord Mallow happened to sing so many duets. There was plenty of time for music during the hour before midnight. After the singing, a rash young gentleman, pining to distinguish himself somehow—a young man with a pimply complexion, who had said with Don Carlos, "Three-and-twenty years of age, and nothing done for immortality"—recited Tennyson's "Farewell to the Old Year," in a voice which was like anything but a trumpet, and with gesticulation painfully suggestive of Saint Vitus.

The long suite of rooms terminated in the orangery, a substantial stone building with tesselated pavement, and wide windows opening on the terrace. The night was wondrously mild. The full moon shed her tender light upon the dark Forest, the shining water-pools, the distant blackness of a group of ancient yew-trees on the crest of a hill. Ashbourne stood high, and the view from the terrace was at all times magnificent, but perhaps finest of all in the moonlight.

The younger guests wandered softly in and out of the rooms, and looked at the golden oranges glimmering against their dark leaves, and put themselves into positions that suggested the possibility of flirtation. Young ladies whose study of German literature had never gone beyond Ollendorff gazed pensively at the oranges, and murmured the song of Mignon. Couples of maturer growth whispered the details of unsavoury scandals behind perfumed fans.

Vixen and Rorie were among these roving couples. Violet had left the piano, and Roderick was off duty. Lady Mabel and Lord Mallow were deep in the wrongs of Ireland. Captain Winstanley was talking agriculture with the Duke, whose mind was sorely exercised about guano.

"My dear sir, in a few years we shall have used up all the guano, and then what can become of us?" demanded the Duke. "Talk about our exhausting our coal! What is that compared with the exhaustion of guano? We may learn to exist without fires. Our winters are becoming milder; our young men are going in for athletics; they can keep themselves warm upon bicycles. And then we have the gigantic coal-fields of America, the vast basin of the Mississippi to fall back upon, with ever-increasing facilities in the mode of transport. But civilisation must come to a deadlock when we have no more guano. Our grass, our turnips, our mangel, must deteriorate, We shall have no more prize cattle. It is too awful to contemplate."

"But do you really consider such a calamity at all probable, Duke?" asked the Captain.

"Probable, sir? It is inevitable. In 1868 the Chincha Islands were estimated to contain about six million tons of guano. The rate of exportation had at that time risen to four hundred thousand tons per annum. At this rate the three islands will be completely exhausted by the year 1888, and England will have to exist without guano. The glory of the English people, as breeders of prize oxen, will have departed."

"Chemistry will have discovered new fertilisers by that time," suggested the Captain, in a comforting tone.

"Sir," replied the Duke severely, "the discoveries of modern science tend to the chimerical rather than the practical. Your modern scientists can liquefy oxygen, they can light a city with electricity, but they cannot give me anything to increase the size and succulence of my turnips. Virgil knew as much about agriculture as your modern chemist."

While the Duke was holding forth about guano, Vixen and Rorie were on the terrace, in the stillness and moonlight. There was hardly a breath of wind. It might have been a summer evening. Vixen was shrouded from head to foot in a white cloak which Rorie had fetched from the room where the ladies had left their wraps. She looked all white and solemn in the moonlight, like a sheeted ghost.

Although Mr. Vawdrey had been civil enough to go in quest of Violet's cloak, and had seemed especially desirous of bringing her to the terrace, he was by no means delightful now he had got her there. They took a turn or two in silence, broken only by a brief remark about the beauty of the night, and the extent of the prospect.

"I think it is the finest view in the Forest," said Vixen, dwelling on the subject for lack of anything else to say. "You must be very fond of Ashbourne."

"I don't exactly recognise the necessity. The view is superb, no doubt; but the house is frightfully commonplace. It is a little better than Briarwood. That is about all which an enthusiastic admirer could advance in its favour. How much longer does Lord Mallow mean to take up his abode with you?"

Vixen shrugged her cloaked shoulders with an action that seemed to express contemptuous carelessness.

"I haven't the least idea. That is no business of mine, you know."

"I don't know anything of the kind," retorted Rorie captiously. "I should have thought it was very much your business."

"Should you, really?" said Vixen mockingly.

If the gentleman's temper was execrable, the lady's mood was not too amiable.

"Yes. Are not you the load-star? It is your presence that makes the Abbey House pleasant to him. Who can wonder that he protracts his stay?"

"He has been with us a little more than a fortnight."

"He has been with you an age. Mortals who are taken up to Paradise seldom stay so long. Sweet dreams are not so long. A fortnight in the same house with you, meeting with you at breakfast, parting with you at midnight, seeing you at noontide and afternoon, walking with you, riding with you, singing with you, kneeling down to family prayer at your side, mixing his 'Amen' with yours; why he might as well be your husband at once. He has as much delight in your society."

"You forget the hours in which he is shooting pheasants and playing billiards."

"Glimpses of purgatory, which make his heaven all the more divine," said Rorie. "Well, it is none of my business, as you said just now. There are people born to be happy, I suppose; creatures that come into the world under a lucky star."

"Undoubtedly, and among them notably Mr. Vawdrey, who has everything that the heart of a reasonable man can desire."

"So had Solomon, and yet he made his moan."

"Oh, there is always a crumpled rose-leaf in everybody's bed. And if the rose-leaves were all smooth, a man would crumple one on purpose, in order to have something to grumble about. Hark, Rorie!" cried Vixen, with a sudden change of tone, as the first silvery chime of Ringwood bells came floating over the woodland distance—the low moon-lit hills; "don't be cross. The old year is dying. Remember the dear days that are gone, when you and I used to think a new year a thing to be glad about. And now, what can the new years bring us half so good as that which the old ones have taken away?"

She had slipped her little gloved hand through his arm, and drawn very near to him, moved by tender thoughts of the past. He looked down at her with eyes from which all anger had vanished. There was only love in them— deep love; love such as a very affectionate brother might perchance give his only sister—but it must be owned that brothers capable of such love are rare.

"No, child," he murmured sadly. "Years to come can bring us nothing so good or so dear as the past. Every new year will drift us farther."

They were standing at the end of the terrace farthest from the orangery windows, out of which the Duchess and her visitors came trooping to hear the Ringwood chimes. Rorie and Vixen kept quite apart from the rest. They stood silent, arm-in-arm, looking across the landscape towards the winding Avon and the quiet market-town, hidden from them by intervening hill. Yonder, nestling among those grassy hills, lies Moyles Court, the good old English manor-house where noble Alice Lisle sheltered the fugitives from Sedgemoor; paying for that one act of womanly hospitality with her life. Farther away, on the banks of the Avon, is the quiet churchyard where that gentle martyr of Jeffreys's lust for blood takes her long rest. The creeping spleenwort thrives amidst the gray stones of her tomb. To Vixen these things were so familiar, that it was as if she could see them with her bodily eyes, as she looked across the distance, with its mysterious shadows, its patches of silver light.

The bells chimed on with their tender cadence, half joyous, half sorrowful. The shallower spirits among the guests chattered about the beauty of the night, and the sweetness of the bells. Deeper souls were silent, full of saddest thoughts. Who is there who has not lost something in the years gone by, which earth's longest future cannot restore? Only eternity can give back the ravished treasures of the dead years.

Violet's lips trembled and were dumb. Roderick saw the tears rolling down her pale cheeks, and offered no word of consolation. He knew that she was thinking of her father.

"Dear old Squire," he murmured gently, after an interval of silence. "How good he was to me, and how fondly I loved him."

That speech was the sweetest comfort he could have offered. Vixen gave his arm a grateful hug.

"Thank God there is someone who remembers him, besides his dogs and me!" she exclaimed; and then she hastily dried her tears, and made herself ready to meet Lord Mallow and Lady Mabel Ashbourne, who were coming along the terrace towards them, talking gaily. Lord Mallow had a much wider range of subjects than Mr. Vawdrey. He had read more, and could keep pace with Lady Mabel in her highest flights; science, literature, politics, were all as one to him. He had crammed his vigorous young mind with everything which it behoved a man panting for parliamentary distinction to know.

"Where have you two people been hiding yourselves for the last half hour?" asked Lady Mabel. "You were wanted badly just now for 'Blow, Gentle Gales.' I know you can manage the bass, Rorie, when you like."

"'Lo, behold a pennant waving!'" sang Rorie in deep full tones. "Yes, I can manage that much, at a push. You seem music mad to-night, Mabel. The old year is making a swan-like end—fading in music."

Rorie and Vixen were still standing arm-in-arm; rather too much as if they belonged to each other, Lady Mabel thought. The attitude was hardly in good taste, according to Lady Mabel's law of taste, which was a code as strict as Draco's.

The bells rang on.

"The new year has come!" cried the Duke. "Let us all shake hands in the friendly German fashion."

On this there was a general shaking of hands, which appeared to last a long time. It seemed rather as if the young people of opposite sexes shook hands with each other more than once. Lord Mallow would hardly let Violet's hand go, once having got it in his hearty grasp.

"Hail to the first new year we greet together," he said softly. "May it not be the last. I feel that it must not, cannot be the last."

"You are wiser than I, then," Vixen answered coldly; "for my feelings tell me nothing about the future—except"—and here her face beamed at him with a lovely smile—"except that you will be kind to Bullfinch."

"If I were an emperor I would make him a consul," answered the Irishman.

He had contrived to separate Roderick and Vixen. The young man had returned to his allegiance, and was escorting Lady Mabel back to the house. Everybody began to feel chilly, now that the bells were silent, and there was a general hurrying off to the carriages, which were standing in an oval ring round a group of deodoras in front of the porch on the other side of the house.

Rorie and Vixen met no more that night. Lord Mallow took her to her carriage, and sat opposite her and talked to her during the homewards drive. Captain Winstanley was smoking a cigar on the box. His wife slumbered peacefully.

"I think I may be satisfied with Theodore," she said, as she composed herself for sleep; "my dress was not quite the worst in the room, was it, Violet?"

"It was lovely, mamma. You can make yourself quite happy," answered Vixen truthfully; whereupon the matron breathed a gentle sigh of content, and lapsed into slumber.

They had the Boldrewood Road before them, a long hilly road cleaving the very heart of the Forest; a road full of ghosts at the best of times, but offering a Walpurgis revel of phantoms on such a night as this to the eye of the belated wanderer. How ghostly the deer were, as they skimmed across the road and flitted away into dim distances, mixing with and melting into the shadows of the trees. The little gray rabbits, sitting up on end, were like circles of hobgoblins that dispersed and vanished at the approach of mortals. The leafless old hawthorns, rugged and crooked, silvered by the moonlight, were most ghostlike of all. They took every form, from the most unearthly to the most grotesquely human.

Violet sat wrapped in her furred white mantle, watching the road as intently as if she had never seen it before. She never could grow tired of these things. She loved them with a love which was part of her nature.

"What a delightful evening, was it not?" asked Lord Mallow.

"I suppose it was very nice," answered Violet coolly; "but I have no standard of comparison. It was my first dinner at Ashbourne."

"What a remarkably clever girl Lady Mabel is. Mr. Vawdrey ought to consider himself extremely fortunate."

"I have never heard him say that he does not so consider himself."

"Naturally. But I think he might be a little more enthusiastic. He is the coolest lover I ever saw."

"Perhaps you judge him by comparison with Irish lovers. Your nation is more demonstrative than ours."

"Oh, an Irish girl would cashier such a fellow as Mr. Vawdrey. But I may possibly misjudge him. You ought to know more about him than I. You have known him——"

"All my life," said Violet simply. "I know that he is good, and stanch and true, that he honoured his mother, and that he will make Lady Mabel Ashbourne a very good husband. Perhaps if she were a little less clever and a little more human, he might be happier with her; but no doubt that will all come right in time."

"Any way it will be all the same in a century or so," assented Lord Mallow. "We are going to have lovely weather as long as this moon lasts, I believe. Will you go for a long ride to-morrow—like that first ride of ours?"

"When I took you all over the world for sport?" said Vixen laughing. "I wonder you are inclined to trust me, after that. If Captain Winstanley likes I don't mind being your guide again to-morrow."

"Captain Winstanley shall like. I'll answer for that. I would make his life unendurable if he were to refuse."

CHAPTER XIII.

Crying for the moon.

Despite the glorious moonlight night which ushered in the new-born year, the first day of that year was abominable; a day of hopeless, incessant rain, falling from a leaden sky in which there was never a break, not a stray gleam of sunshine from morn till eve.

"The new year is like Shakespeare's Richard," said Lord Mallow, when he stood in the porch after breakfast, surveying the horizon. "'Tetchy and wayward was his infancy.' I never experienced anything so provoking. I was dreaming all night of our ride."

"Were you not afraid of being like that dreadful man in 'Locksley Hall'?—

Like a dog, he hunts in dreams,"

asked Vixen mockingly.

She was standing on the threshold, playing with Argus, looking the picture of healthful beauty, in her dark green cloth dress and plain linen collar. All Vixen's morning costumes were of the simplest and neatest; a compact style of dress which interfered with none of her rural amusements. She could romp with her dog, make her round of the stables, work in the garden, ramble in the Forest, without fear of dilapidated flounces or dishevelled laces and ribbons.

"Violet's morning-dresses are so dreadfully strong-minded," complained Mrs. Winstanley. "To look at her, one would almost think that she was the kind of girl to go round the country lecturing upon woman's rights."

"No ride this morning," said Captain Winstanley, coming into the hall, with a bundle of letters in his hand. "I shall go to my den, and do a morning's letter-writing and accountancy—unless you want me for a shy at the pheasants, Mallow?"

"Let the pheasants be at rest for the first day of the year," answered Lord Mallow. "I am sure you would rather be fetching up your arrears of correspondence than shooting at dejected birds in a damp plantation; and I am luxurious enough to prefer staying indoors, if the ladies will have me. I can help Miss Tempest to wind her wools."

"Thanks, but I never do any wool-work. Mamma is the artist in that line."

"Then I place myself unreservedly at Mrs. Winstanley's feet."

"You are too good," sighed the fair matron, from her arm-chair by the hearth; "but I shall not touch my crewels to-day. I have one of my nervous headaches. It is a penalty I too often have to pay for the pleasures of society. I'm afraid I shall have to lie down for an hour or two."

And with a languid sigh Mrs. Winstanley wrapped her China crape shawl round her, and went slowly upstairs, leaving Violet and Lord Mallow in sole possession of the great oak-panelled hall; the lady looking at the rain from her favourite perch in the deep window-seat, the gentleman contemplating the same prospect from the open door. It was one of those mild winter mornings when a huge wood fire is a cheerful feature in the scene, but hardly essential to comfort.

Vixen thought of that long rainy day, years ago, the day on which Roderick Vawdrey came of age. How well she remembered sitting in that very window, watching the ceaseless rain, with a chilly sense of having been forgotten and neglected by her old companion. And then, in the gloaming, just when she had lost all hope of seeing him, he had come leaping in out of the wet night, like a lion from his lair, and had taken her in his arms and kissed her before she knew what he was doing.

Her cheeks crimsoned even to-day at the memory of that kiss. It had seemed a small thing then. Now it seemed awful—a burning spot of shame upon the whiteness of her youth.

"He must have thought I was very fond of him, or he would not have dared to treat me so," she told herself. "But then we had been playfellows so long. I had teased him, and he had plagued me; and we had been really like brother and sister. Poor Rorie! If we could have always been young we should have been better friends."

"How thoughtful you seem this morning, Miss Tempest," said a voice behind Vixen's shoulder.

"Do I?" she asked, turning quickly round. "New Year's Day is a time to make one thoughtful. It is like beginning a new chapter in the volume of life, and one cannot help speculating as to what the chapter is to be about."

"For you it ought to be a story full of happiness."

"Ah, but you don't know my history. I had such a happy childhood. I drained my cup of bliss before I was a woman, and there is nothing left for me but the dregs, and they—they are dust and ashes."

There was an intensity of bitterness in her tone that moved him beyond his power of self-control. That she—so fair, so lovely, so deeply dear to him already; she for whom life should be one summer-day of unclouded gladness —that she should give expression to a rooted sorrow was more than his patience could bear.

"Violet, you must not speak thus; you wound me to the heart. Oh, my love, my love, you were born to be the giver of gladness, the centre of joy and delight. Grief should never touch you; sorrow and pain should never come near you. You are a creature of happiness and light."

"Don't!" cried Vixen vehemently. "Oh, pray don't. It is all vain—useless. My life is marked out for me. No one can alter it. Pray do not lower yourself by one word more. You will be sorry—angry with yourself and me— afterwards."

"Violet, I must speak."

"To what end? My fate is as fixed as the stars. No one can change it."

"No mortal perhaps, Violet. But Love can. Love is a god. Oh, my darling, I have learnt to love you dearly and fondly in this little while, and I mean to win you. It shall go hard with me if I do not succeed. Dear love, if truth and constancy can conquer fate, I ought to be able to win you. There is no one else, is there, Violet?" he asked falteringly, with his eyes upon her downcast face.

A burning spot glowed and faded on her cheek before she answered him.

"Can you not see how empty my life is?" she asked with a bitter laugh. "No; there is no one else. I stand quite alone. Death took my father from me; your friend has robbed me of my mother. My old playfellow, Roderick Vawdrey, belongs to his cousin. I belong to nobody."

"Let me have you then, Violet. Ah, if you knew how I would cherish you! You should be loved so well that you would fancy yourself the centre of the universe, and that all the planets revolved in the skies only to please you. Love, let me have you—priceless treasure that others know not how to value. Let me keep and guard you."

"I would not wrong you so much as to marry you without loving you, and I shall never love any more," said Vixen, with a sad steadfastness that was more dispiriting than the most vehement protestation.

"Why not?"

"Because I spent all my store of love while I was a child. I loved my father —ah, I cannot tell you how fondly. I do not think there are many fathers who are loved as he was. I poured out all my treasures of affection at his feet. I have no love left for a husband."

"What, Violet, not if your old friend Roderick Vawdrey were pleading?" asked Lord Mallow.

It was an unlucky speech. If Lord Mallow had had a chance, which he had not, that speech would have spoiled it. Violet started to her feet, her cheeks crimson, her eyes flashing.

"It is shameful, abominable of you to say such a thing!" she cried, her voice tremulous with indignation. "I will never forgive you for that dastardly speech. Come, Argus."

She had mounted the broad oak stairs with light swift foot before Lord Mallow could apologise. He was terribly crestfallen.

"I was a brute," he muttered to himself. "But I hit the bull's-eye. It is that fellow she loves. Hard upon me, when I ask for nothing but to be her slave and adore her all the days of my life. And I know that Winstanley would have been pleased. How lovely she looked when she was angry—her tawny hair gleaming in the firelight, her great brown eyes flashing. Yes, it's the Hampshire squire she cares for, and I'm out of it. I'll go and shoot the pheasants," concluded Lord Mallow savagely; "those beggars shall not have it all their own way to-day."

He went off to get his gun, in the worst humour he had ever been in since he was a child and cried for the moon.

He spent the whole day in a young oak plantation, ankle-deep in oozy mud, moss, and dead fern, making havoc among the innocent birds. He was in so bloodthirsty a temper, that he felt as if he could have shot a covey of young children, had they come in his way, with all the ferocity of a modern Herod.

"I think I've spoiled Winstanley's coverts for this year, at any rate," he said to himself, as he tramped homewards in the early darkness, with no small hazard of losing himself in one of those ghostly plantations, which were all exactly alike, and in which a man might walk all day long without meeting anything nearer humanity than a trespassing forest pony that had leapt a fence in quest of more sufficing food than the scanty herbage of the open woods.

Lord Mallow got on better than might have been expected. He went east when he ought to have gone west, and found himself in Queen's Bower when he fancied himself in Gretnam Wood; but he did not walk more than half-a-dozen miles out of his way, and he got home somehow at last, which was much for a stranger to the ground.

The stable clock was chiming the quarter before six when he went into the hall, where Vixen had left him in anger that morning. The great wood fire was burning gaily, and Captain Winstanley was sitting in a Glastonbury chair in front of it. "Went for the birds after all, old fellow," he said, without looking round, recognising the tread of Lord Mallow's shooting-boots. "You found it too dismal in the house, I suppose? Consistently abominable weather, isn't it? You must be soaked to the skin."

"I suppose I am," answered the other carelessly. "But I've been soaked a good many times before, and it hasn't done me much harm. Thanks to the modern inventions of the waterproof-makers, the soaking begins inside instead of out. I should call myself parboiled."

"Take off your oilskins and come and talk. You'll have a nip, won't you?" added Captain Winstanley, ringing the bell. "Kirschenwasser, curaçoa, Glenlivat—which shall it be?"

"Glenlivat," answered Lord Mallow, "and plenty of it. I'm in the humour in which a man must either drink inordinately or cut his throat."

"Were the birds unapproachable?" asked Captain Winstanley, laughing; "or were the dogs troublesome?"

"Birds and dogs were perfect; but—— Well, I suppose I'd better make a clean breast of it. I've had a capital time here—— Oh, here comes the whisky. Hold your hand, old fellow!" cried Lord Mallow, as his host poured the Glenlivat somewhat recklessly into a soda-water tumbler. "You mustn't take

99

me too literally. Just moisten the bottom of the glass with whisky before you put in the soda. That's as much as I care about."

"All right. You were saying——"

"That my visit here has been simply delightful, and that I must go to London by an early train to-morrow."

"Paradoxical!" remarked the Captain. "That sounds like your well-bred servant, who tells you that he has nothing to say against the situation, but he wishes to leave you at the end of his month. What's the matter, dear boy? Do you find our Forest hermitage too dull?"

"I should ask nothing kinder from Fate than to be allowed to spend my days in your Forest. Yes, I would say good-bye to the green hills and vales of County Cork, and become that detestable being, an absentee, if—if—Fortune smiled on me. But she doesn't, you see, and I must go. Perhaps you may have perceived, Winstanley—perhaps you may not have been altogether averse from the idea—in a word, I have fallen over head and ears in love with your bewitching stepdaughter."

"My dear fellow, I'm delighted. It is the thing I would have wished, had I been bold enough to wish for anything so good. And of course Violet is charmed. You are the very man for her."

"Am I? So I thought myself till this morning. Unfortunately the young lady is of a different opinion. She has refused me."

"Refused you! Pshaw, they all begin that way. It's one of the small diplomacies of the sex. They think they enhance their value by an assumed reluctance. Nonsense, man, try again. She can't help liking you."

"I would try again, every day for a twelvemonth, if there were a scintilla of hope. My life should be a series of offers. But the thing is decided. I know from her manner, from her face, that I have no chance. I have been in the habit of thinking myself rather a nice kind of fellow, and the women have encouraged the idea. But I don't answer here, Winstanley. Miss Tempest will have nothing to say to me."

"She's a fool," said Captain Winstanley, with his teeth set, and that dark look of his which meant harm to somebody. "I'll talk to her."

"My dear Winstanley, understand I'll have no coercion. If I win her, I must do it off my own bat. Dearly as I love her, if you were to bring her to me conquered and submissive, like Iphigenia at the altar, I would not have her. I love her much too well to ask any sacrifice of inclination from her. I love her too well to accept anything less than her free unfettered heart. She cannot give me that, and I must go. I had much rather you should say nothing about me, either to her or her mother."

"But I shall say a great deal to both," exclaimed the Captain, desperately angry. "I am indignant. I am outraged by her conduct. What in Heaven's name does this wilful girl want in a husband? You have youth, good looks, good temper, talent, tastes that harmonise with her own. You can give her a finer position than she has any right to expect. And she refuses you. She is a spoiled child, who doesn't know her own mind or her own advantage. She has a diabolical temper, and is as wild as a hawk. Egad, I congratulate you on your escape, Mallow. She was not born to make any man happy."

"Small thanks for your congratulations," retorted the Irishman. "She might have made me happy if she had chosen. I would have forgiven her tempers, and loved her for her wildness. She is the sweetest woman I ever knew; as fresh and fair as your furzy hill-tops. But she is not for me. Fate never meant me to be so blessed."

"She will change her mind before she is many months older," said Captain Winstanley. "Her father and mother have spoilt her. She is a creature of whims and fancies, and must be ridden on the curb."

"I would ride her with the lightest snaffle-bit that ever was made," protested Lord Mallow. "But there's no use in talking about it. You won't think me discourteous or ungrateful if I clear out of this to-morrow morning, will you, Winstanley?"

"Certainly not," answered his host; "but I shall think you a confounded ass. Why not wait and try your luck again?"

"Simply because I know it would be useless. Truth and candour shine in that girl's eyes. She has a soul above the petty trickeries of her sex. No from her lips means No, between this and eternity. Oh, thrice blessed will that man be to whom she answers Yes; for she will give him the tenderest, truest, most generous heart in creation."

"You answer boldly for her on so short an acquaintance."

"I answer as a man who loves her, and who has looked into her soul," replied Lord Mallow. "You and she don't hit it over well, I fancy."

"No. We began by disliking each other, and we have been wonderfully constant to our first opinions."

"I can't understand——"

"Can't you? You will, perhaps, some day: if you ever have a handsome stepdaughter who sets up her back against you from the beginning of things.

Have you ever seen a sleek handsome tabby put herself on the defensive at the approach of a terrier, her back arched, her eyes flashing green lightnings, her tail lashing itself, her whiskers bristling? That's my stepdaughter's attitude towards me, and I daresay before long I shall feel her claws. There goes the gong, and we must go too. I'm sorry Miss Tempest has been such a fool, Mallow; but I must repeat my congratulations, even at the risk of offending you."

There were no duets that evening. Vixen was as cold as ice, and as silent as a statue. She sat in the shadow of her mother's arm-chair after dinner, turning over the leaves of Doré's "Tennyson," pausing to contemplate Elaine with a half-contemptuous pity—a curious feeling that hurt her like a physical pain.

"Poor wretch!" she mused. "Are there women in our days so weak as to love where they can never be loved again, I wonder? It is foolish enough in a man; but he cures himself as quickly as the mungoose that gets bitten by a snake, and runs away to find the herb which is an antidote to the venom, and comes back ready to fight the snake again."

"Are we not going to have any music?" asked Mrs. Winstanley languidly, more interested in the *picots* her clever needle was executing on a piece of Italian point than in the reply. "Lord Mallow, cannot you persuade Violet to join you in one of those sweet duets of Mendelssohn's?"

"Indeed, mamma, I couldn't sing a note. I'm as husky as a raven."

"I'm not surprised to hear it," said the Captain, looking up from his study of *The Gardener's Chronicle*. "No doubt you managed to catch cold last night, while you were mooning upon the terrace with young Vawdrey."

"How very incautious of you, Violet!" exclaimed Mrs. Winstanley, in her complaining tone.

"I was not cold, mamma; I had my warm cloak."

"But you confess you have caught cold. I detest colds; they always go through a house. I shall be the next victim, I daresay; and with me a cold is martyrdom. I'm afraid you must find us very dull, Lord Mallow, for New Year's Day, when people expect to be lively. We ought to have had a dinner-party."

"My dear Mrs. Winstanley, I don't care a straw about New Year's Day, and I am not in a lively vein. This quiet evening suits me much better than high jinks, I assure you."

"It's very good of you to say so."

"Come and play a game of billiards," said Captain Winstanley, throwing down his paper.

"Upon my honour, I'd rather sit by the fire and watch Mrs. Winstanley at her point-lace. I'm in an abominably lazy mood after my tramp in those soppy plantations." answered Lord Mallow, who felt a foolish pleasure—mingled with bitterest regrets—in being in the same room with the girl he loved.

She was hidden from him in her shadowy corner; shrouded on one side by the velvet drapery of the fireplace, on the other by her mother's chair. He could only catch a glimpse of her auburn plaits now and then as her head bent over her open book. He never heard her voice, or met her eyes. And yet it was sweet to him to sit in the same room with her.

"Come, Mallow, you can sing us something, at any rate," said the Captain, suppressing a yawn. "I know you can play your own accompaniment, when you please. You can't be too idle to give us one of Moore's melodies."

"I'll sing, if you like, Mrs. Winstanley," assented Lord Mallow, "but I'm afraid you must be tired of my songs. My *répertoire* is rather limited."

"Your songs are charming," said Mrs. Winstanley.

The Irishman seated himself at the distant piano, struck a chord or two, and began the old melody, with its familiar refrain:

> Oh, there's nothing half so sweet in life
> As love's young dream.

Before his song was finished Violet had kissed her mother and glided silently from the room, Lord Mallow saw her go, and there was a sudden break in his voice as the door closed upon her, a break that sounded almost like a suppressed sob.

When Vixen came down to breakfast next morning she found the table laid only for three.

"What has become of Lord Mallow?" she asked Forbes, when he brought in the urn.

"He left by an early train, ma'am. Captain Winstanley drove him to Lyndhurst."

The old servants of the Abbey House had not yet brought themselves to speak of their new lord as "master." He was always "Captain Winstanley."

The Captain came in while Violet knelt by the fire playing with Argus, whom even the new rule had not banished wholly from the family sitting-rooms.

The servants filed in for morning prayers, which Captain Winstanley delivered in a cold hard voice. His manual of family worship was of concise and businesslike form, and the whole ceremony lasted about seven minutes. Then the household dispersed quickly, and Forbes brought in his tray of covered dishes.

"You can pour out the tea, Violet. Your mother is feeling a little tired, and will breakfast in her room."

"Then I think, if you'll excuse me, I'll have my breakfast with her," said Vixen. "She'll be glad of my company, I daresay."

"She has a headache and will be better alone. Stop where you are, if you please, Violet. I have something serious to say to you."

Vixen left off pouring out the tea, clasped her hands in her lap, and looked at Captain Winstanley with the most resolute expression he had ever seen in a woman's face.

"Are you going to talk to me about Lord Mallow?" she asked.

"Yes."

"Then spare yourself the trouble. It would be useless."

"I cannot conceive that you should be so besotted as to refuse a man who offers so much. A man who has wealth, rank, youth, good looks——"

"Spare me the catalogue of your friend's merits. I think him a most estimable person. I acknowledge his rank and wealth. But I have refused him."

"You will change your mind."

"I never change my mind."

"You will live to repent your folly then, Miss Tempest: and all I hope is that your remorse may be keen. It is not one woman in a thousand who gets such a chance. What are you that you should throw it away?"

"I am a woman who would sooner cut my throat than marry a man I cannot honestly love," answered Vixen, with unblenching firmness.

"I think I understand your motive," said Captain Winstanley. "Lord Mallow never had a chance with you. The ground was occupied before he came. You are a very foolish girl to reject so good an offer for the sake of another woman's sweetheart."

"How dare you say that to me?" cried Vixen. "You have usurped my father's place; you have robbed me of my mother's heart. Is not that cause enough for me to hate you? I have only one friend left in the world, Roderick Vawdrey. And you would slander me because I cling to that old friendship, the last remnant of my happy childhood."

"You might have a dozen such friends, if friendship is all you want, and be Lady Mallow into the bargain," retorted Captain Winstanley scornfully. "You are a simpleton to send such a man away despairing. But I suppose it is idle to ask you to hear reason. I am not your father, and even if I were, I daresay you would take your own way in spite of me."

"My father would not have asked me to marry a man I did not love," answered Vixen proudly, her eyes clouding with tears even at the thought of her beloved dead; "and he would have valued Lord Mallow's rank and fortune no more than I do. But you are so fond of a bargain," she added, her eye kindling and her lip curving with bitterest scorn. "You sold Bullfinch, and now you want to sell me."

"By Heaven, madam, I pity the man who may be fool enough to buy you!" cried the Captain, starting up from his untasted breakfast, and leaving Vixen mistress of the field.

CHAPTER XIV.

"Kurz ist der Schmerz und ewig ist die Freude."

Captain Winstanley said no more about Lord Mallow; but Violet had to listen to much plaintive bemoaning from her mother, who could not understand how any well-brought-up young woman could refuse an Irish peer with a fine estate, and the delights of a *trousseau* made by the renowned Theodore. Upon this latter detail Mrs. Winstanley dwelt at more length than upon that minor circumstance in a marriage—the bridegroom.

"It would have been such a pleasure to me to plan your *trousseau*, darling," she said; "such an occupation for my mind in these wretched winter afternoons when there is no possibility of driving or making calls. I should have attended to everything myself. Theodore's general way is to make a list of what she thinks necessary, allowing her customer to correct it; but I should not have been satisfied with that, even from Theodore, though I admit that her taste is perfect. And then, you know, she is hand in glove with Worth, and that alone is a liberal education, as somebody says somewhere about something.

No, dear, I would have done it all myself. I know the exact shades that suit your complexion, the dashes of colour that contrast with and light up your hair, the style that sets off your figure. Your *trousseau* should be talked about in society, and even described in the fashion magazines. And then Lord Mallow is really so very nice—and has such a charming baritone—what more can you want?"

"Only to love him, mamma dearest, which I do not, and never shall. That frank loud voice of his does not stir a fibre of my heart. I like him extremely, and so I do Mr. Scobel, and Bates the groom. Lord Mallow is no more to me than either of those. Indeed, Bates is much nearer and dearer, for he loved my father."

"My dear Violet, you have the most republican ideas. Imagine anyone putting Bates on a level with Lord Mallow!"

"I don't, mamma. I only say he is more to me than Lord Mallow could ever be."

"Your travelling-dress," murmured Mrs. Winstanley, her mind still dwelling on the *trousseau;* "that affords more scope for taste than the wedding-gown. Velvet suits your style, but is too heavy for your age. A soft clinging cashmere, now, one of those delicious neutral tints that have been so fashionable lately, over an underskirt of a warmer colour in *poult de soie*, a picturesque costume that would faintly recall Lely's portraits at Hampton Court."

"Dear mamma, what is the use of talking about dresses I am never going to require? Not for all the finery that Theodore ever made would I marry Lord Mallow, or anybody else. I am happy enough with you, and my horse, and my dog, and all the dear old things, animal and vegetable, that belong to this dear old place. I shall never leave you, or the Forest. Can you not be content to know this and let me alone?"

"You are a very wilful girl, Violet, and ridiculously blind to your own interests," remarked Mrs. Winstanley, throwing herself back in her chair with a fretful look, "and you put me in an absurd position. The duchess quite congratulated me about your brilliant prospects, when we were chatting together on New Year's Eve. Anybody could see how devoted Lord Mallow was, she said, and what a splendid match it would be for you."

"Let the Duchess marry her own daughter, and leave me alone," cried Vixen scornfully.

This was the kind of thing she had to endure continually during the chill winter months that followed Lord Mallow's departure. Even her old friends the Scobels worried her about the Irish peer, and lamented her inability to perceive his merits. It was known throughout her particular circle that she had been idiotic enough to refuse Lord Mallow. Mrs. Winstanley had whispered the fact to all her friends, under the seal of strictest secrecy. Of all Vixen's acquaintance, Roderick Vawdrey was the only one who said no word to her about Lord Mallow; but he was much kinder to her after the Irishman's departure than he had shown himself during his visit.

Spring put on her green mantle; and when the woods were starred with primroses, and the banks lovely with heaven-hued dog-violets, everyone of any pretension to importance in the social scale began to flee from the Forest as from a loathsome place. Lord Ellangowan's train of vans and waggons set out for the railway-station with their load of chests and baskets. Julius Caesar's baggage was as nothing to the Saratoga trunks and bonnet-boxes of Lady Ellangowan. The departure of the Israelites from Egypt was hardly a mightier business than this emigration of the Ellangowan household. The Duke and Duchess, and Lady Mabel Ashbourne, left for the Queen Anne house at Kensington, whereat the fashionable London papers broke out in paragraphs of rejoicing, and the local journals bewailed the extinction of their sun.

The London season had begun, and only the nobodies stayed in the Forest to watch the rosy sunsets glow and fade behind the yellow oaks; to see the purple of the beech-boughs change mysteriously to brightest green; and the bluebells burst into blossom in the untrodden glades and bottoms. Captain Winstanley found a small house in Mayfair, which he hired for six weeks, at a rent which he pronounced exorbitant. He sacrificed his own ideas of prudence to the gratification of his wife; who had made up her mind that she had scarcely the right to exist until she had been presented to her sovereign in her new name. But when Mrs. Winstanley ventured to suggest the Duchess of Dovedale, as her sponsor on this solemn occasion, her husband sternly tabooed the notion.

"My aunt, Lady Susan Winstanley, is the proper person to present you," he said authoritatively.

"But is she really your aunt, Conrad? You never mentioned her before we were married?"

"She is my father's third cousin by marriage; but we have always called her Aunt. She is the widow of Major-General Winstanley, who distinguished himself in the last war with Tippoo Saïb, and had a place at Court in the reign of William the Fourth."

"She must be dreadfully old and dowdy," sighed Mrs. Winstanley, whose only historical idea of the Sailor King's reign was as a period of short waists and beaver bonnets.

"She is not a chicken, and she does not spend eight hundred a year on her dressmaker," retorted the Captain. "But she is a very worthy woman, and highly respected by her friends. Why should you ask a favour of the Duchess of Dovedale?"

"Her name would look so well in the papers," pleaded Mrs. Winstanley.

"The name of your husband's kinswoman will look much more respectable," answered the Captain; and in this, as in most matters, he had his own way.

Lady Susan Winstanley was brought from her palatial retirement to spend a fortnight in Mayfair. She was bony, wiggy, and snuffy; wore false teeth and seedy apparel; but she was well-bred and well-informed, and Vixen got on with her much better than with the accomplished Captain. Lady Susan took to Vixen; and these two went out for early walks together in the adjacent Green Park, and perambulated the picture-galleries, before Mrs. Winstanley had braced herself up for the fatigues of a fashionable afternoon.

Sometimes they came across Mr. Vawdrey at a picture-gallery or in the Park; and at the first of these chance meetings, struck by the obvious delight with which the two young people greeted each other, Lady Susan jumped to a conclusion.

"That's your young man, I suppose, my dear," she said bluntly, when Rorie had left them.

"Oh, Lady Susan!"

"It's a vulgar expression, I know, my dear, but it comes natural to me; I hear it so often from our housemaids. I fancied that you and that handsome young fellow must be engaged."

"Oh no. We are only old friends. He is engaged to Lady Mabel Ashbourne —a very grand match."

"That's a pity," said Lady Susan.

"Why?"

"Well, my dear," answered the old lady hesitatingly, "because when one hears of a grand match, it generally means that a young man is marrying for the sake of money, and that young old friend of yours looks too good to throw himself away like that."

"Oh, but indeed, Lady Susan, it is not so in Rorie's case. He has plenty of money of his own."

The important day came; and Lady Susan, Mrs. Winstanley, and Violet packed themselves and their finery into a capacious carriage, and set off for St. James's. The fair Pamela's costume was an elaborate example of Theodore's highest art; colours, design, all of the newest—a delicate harmony of half-tints, an indescribable interblending of feathers, lace, and flowers. Violet was simply and elegantly dressed by the same great artist. Lady Susan wore a petticoat and train that must have been made in the time of Queen Adelaide. Yes, the faded and unknown hue of the substantial brocade, the skimpiness of the satin, the quaint devices in piping-cord and feather-stitch—must assuredly have been coeval with that good woman's famous hat and spencer.

Poor Mrs. Winstanley was horrified when she saw her husband's kinswoman attired for the ceremony, not a whit less wiggy and snuffy than usual, and with three lean ostrich feathers starting erect from her back hair, like the ladies in the proscenium boxes of Skelt's Theatre, whose gaily painted effigies were so dear to our childhood.

Poor Pamela felt inclined to shed tears. Even her confidence in the perfection of her own toilet could hardly sustain her against the horror of being presented by such a scarecrow.

The ceremony went off satisfactorily, in spite of Lady Susan's antiquated garments. Nobody laughed. Perhaps the *habitués* of St. James's were accustomed to scarecrows. Violet's fresh young beauty attracted some little notice as she waited among the crowd of *débutantes;* but, on its being ascertained that she was nobody in particular, curiosity languished and died.

Mrs. Winstanley wanted to exhibit her court-dress at the opera that evening, but her husband protested against this display as bad style. Vixen was only too glad to throw off her finery, the tulle puffings and festoonings, and floral wreaths and bouquets, which made movement difficult and sitting down almost impossible.

Those six weeks in town were chiefly devoted to gaiety. Mrs. Winstanley's Hampshire friends called on her, and followed up their calls by invitations to dinner, and at the dinners she generally met people who were on the eve of giving a garden-party, or a concert, or a dance, and who begged to be allowed to send her a card for that entertainment, spoken of modestly as a thing of no account. And then there was a hurried interchange of calls, and Violet found herself meandering about an unknown croquet-lawn, amongst unknown nobodies, under a burning sun, looking at other girls, dressed like herself in dresses à la Theodore, with the last thing in sleeves, and the last cut in trains, all pretending to be amused by the vapid and languid observations of the cavalier told off to them, paired like companions of the chain at Toulon, and almost as joyous.

Violet Tempest attended no less than eight private concerts during those six weeks, and heard the same new ballad, and the same latest gavotte in C minor, at everyone of them. She was taken to pianoforte recitals in fashionable squares and streets, and heard Bach and Beethoven till her heart ached with pity for the patient labour of the performers, knowing how poorly she and the majority of mankind appreciated their efforts. She went to a few dances that were rather amusing, and waltzed to her heart's content. She rode Arion in the Row, and horse and rider were admired as perfect after then kind. Once she met Lord Mallow, riding beside Lady Mabel Ashbourne and the Duke of Dovedale. His florid cheek paled a little at the sight of her. They passed each other with a friendly bow, and this was their only meeting. Lord Mallow left cards at the house in Mayfair a week before the Winstanleys went back to Hampshire. He had been working hard at his senatorial duties, and had made some telling speeches upon the Irish land question. People talked of him as a rising politician; and, whenever his name appeared in the morning papers, Mrs. Winstanley uplifted her voice at the breakfast-table, and made her wail about Violet's folly in refusing such an excellent young man.

"It would have been so nice to be able to talk about my daughter, Lady Mallow, and Castle Mallow," said Pamela in confidence to her husband.

"No doubt, my dear," he answered coolly; "but when you bring up a young woman to have her own way in everything, you must take the consequences."

"It is very ungrateful of Violet," sighed the afflicted mother, "after the pains I have taken to dress her prettily, ever since she was a baby. It is a very poor return for my care."

CHAPTER XV.

A Midsummer Night's Dream.

They were all back at the Abbey House again early in June, and Vixen breathed more freely in her sweet native air. How dear, how doubly beautiful, everything seemed to her after even so brief an exile. But it was a grief to have missed the apple-bloom and the bluebells. The woods were putting on their ripe summer beauty; the beeches had lost the first freshness of their tender green, the amber glory of the young oak-leaves was over, the last of the primroses had paled and faded among the spreading bracken; masses of snowy hawthorn bloom gleamed white amidst the woodland shadows; bean-fields in full bloom filled the air with delicate odours; the summer winds swept across the long lush grass in the meadows, beautiful with ever-varying lights and shadows; families of sturdy black piglings were grubbing on the waste turf beside every road, and the forest-fly was getting strong upon the wing. The depths of Mark Ash were dark at noontide under their roof of foliage.

Vixen revelled in the summer weather. She was out from morning till evening, on foot or on horseback, sketching or reading a novel, in some solitary corner of the woods, with Argus for her companion and guardian. It was an idle purposeless existence for a young woman to lead, no doubt; but Violet Tempest knew of no better thing that life offered her to do.

Neither her mother nor Captain Winstanley interfered with her liberty. The Captain had his own occupations and amusements, and his wife was given up to frivolities which left no room in her mind for anxiety about her only daughter. So long as Violet looked fresh and pretty at the breakfast-table, and was nicely dressed in the evening, Mrs. Winstanley thought that all was well; or at least as well as it ever could be with a girl who had been so besotted as to refuse a wealthy young nobleman. So Vixen went her own way, and nobody cared. She seemed to have a passion for solitude, and avoided even her old friends, the Scobels, who had made themselves odious by their championship of Lord Mallow.

The London season was at its height when the Winstanleys went back to Hampshire. The Dovedales were to be at Kensington till the beginning of July, with Mr. Vawdrey in attendance upon them. He had rooms in Ebury Street, and had assumed an urban air which in Vixen's opinion made him execrable.

"I can't tell you how hateful you look in lavender gloves and a high hat," she said to him one day in Clarges Street.

"I daresay I look more natural dressed like a gamekeeper," he answered lightly; "I was born so. As for the high hat, you can't hate it more than I do; and I have always considered gloves a foolishness on a level with pigtails and hair-powder."

Vixen had been wandering in her old haunts for something less than a fortnight, when, on one especially fine morning, she mounted Arion directly after breakfast and started on one of her rambles, with the faithful Bates in attendance, to open gates or to pull her out of bogs if needful. Upon this point Mrs. Winstanley was strict. Violet might ride when and where she pleased—since these meanderings in the Forest were so great a pleasure to her—but she must never ride without a groom.

Old Bates liked the duty. He adored his mistress, and had spent the greater part of his life in the saddle. There was no more enjoyable kind of idleness possible for him than to jog along in the sunshine on one of the Captain's old hunters; called upon for no greater exertion than to flick an occasional fly off his horse's haunch, or to bend down and hook open the gate of a plantation with his stout hunting-crop. Bates had many a brief snatch of slumber in those warm enclosures, where the air was heavy with the scent of the pines, and the buzzing of summer flies made a perpetual lullaby. There was a delicious sense of repose in such a sleep, but it was not quite so pleasant to be jerked suddenly into the waking world by a savage plunge of the aggravated hunter's hindlegs, goaded to madness by a lively specimen of the forest-fly.

On this particular morning Vixen was in a thoughtful mood, and Arion was lazy. She let him walk at a leisurely pace under the beeches of Gretnam Wood, and through the quiet paths of the New Park plantations. He came slowly out into Queen's Bower, tossing his delicate head and sniffing the summer air. The streamlets were rippling gaily in the noontide sun; far off on the yellow common a solitary angler was whipping the stream—quite an unusual figure in the lonely landscape. A delicious slumberous quiet reigned over all the scene. Vixen was lost in thought, Bates was dreaming, when a horse's hoofs came up stealthily beside Arion, and a manly voice startled the sultry stillness.

"I've got rid of the high hat for this year, and I'm my own man again," said the voice; and then a strong brown hand was laid upon Vixen's glove, and swallowed up her slender fingers in its warm grasp.

"When did you come back?" she asked, as soon as their friendly greetings were over, and Arion had reconciled himself to the companionship of Mr. Vawdrey's hack.

"Late last night."

"And have the Duchess and her people come back to Ashbourne?"

"*Pas si bête.* The Duchess and her people—meaning Mabel—have engagements six deep for the next month—breakfasts, lawn-parties, music, art, science, horticulture, dancing, archery, every form of labourious amusement that the genius of man has invented. One of our modern sages has said that life would be tolerable but for its amusements. I am of that wise man's opinion. Fashionable festivities are my aversion. So I told Mabel frankly that I found my good spirits being crushed out of me by the weight of too much pleasure, and that I must come home to look after my farm. The dear old Duke recognised that duty immediately, and gave me all sorts of messages and admonitions for his bailiff."

"And you are really free to do what you like for a month?" exclaimed Vixen naïvely. "Poor Rorie! How glad you must be!"

"My liberty is of even greater extent. I am free till the middle of August, when I am to join the Dovedales in Scotland. Later, I suppose, the Duke will go to Baden, or to some newly-discovered fountain in the Black Forest. He could not exist for a twelvemonth without German waters."

"And after that there will be a wedding, I suppose?" said Violet.

She felt as if called upon to say something of this kind. She wanted Rorie to know that she recognised his position as an engaged man. She hated talking about the business, but she felt somehow that this was incumbent upon her.

"I suppose so," answered Rorie; "a man must be married once in his life. The sooner he gets the ceremony over the better. My engagement has hung fire rather. There is always a kind of flatness about the thing between cousins, I daresay. Neither of us is in a hurry. Mabel has so many ideas and occupations, from orchids to Greek choruses."

"She is very clever," said Vixen.

"She is clever and good, and I am very proud of her," answered Rorie loyally.

He felt as if he were walking on the brink of a precipice, and that it needed all his care to steer clear of the edge.

After this there was no more said about Lady Mabel. Vixen and Rorie rode on happily side by side, as wholly absorbed in each other as Launcelot and Guinevere—when the knight brought the lady home through the smiling land, in the glad boyhood of the year, by tinkling rivulet and shadowy covert, and twisted ivy and spreading chestnut fans—and with no more thought of Lady Mabel than those two had of King Arthur.

It was the first of many such rides in the fair June weather. Vixen and Rorie were always meeting in that sweet pathless entanglement of oak and beech and holly, where the cattle-line of the spreading branches were just high enough to clear Vixen's coquettish little hat, or in the long straight fir plantations, where the light was darkened even at noonday, and where the slumberous stillness was broken only by the hum of summer flies. It was hardly possible, it seemed to Violet, for two people to be always riding in the Forest without meeting each other very often. Various as the paths are they all cross somewhere: and what more natural than to see Rorie's brown horse trotting calmly along the grass by the wayside, at the first bend of the road? They made no appointments, or were not conscious of making any; but they always met. There was a fatality about it: yet neither Rorie nor Violet ever seemed surprised at this persistence of fate. They were always glad to see each other; they had always a world to tell each other. If the earth had been newly made every day, with a new set of beings to people it, those two could hardly have had more to say.

"Darned if I can tell what our young Miss and Muster Vawdrey can find to talk about," said honest old Bates, over his dish of tea in the servants' hall; "but their tongues ha' never done wagging."

Sometimes Miss Tempest and Mr. Vawdrey went to the kennels together, and idled away an hour with the hounds; while their horses stood at ease with their bridles looped round the five-barred gate, their heads hanging lazily over the topmost bar, and their big soft eyes dreamily contemplating the opposite pine wood, with that large capacity for perfect idleness common to their species. Bates was chewing a straw and swinging his hunting-crop somewhere in attendance. He went with his young mistress everywhere, and played the part of the "dragon of prudery placed within call;" but he was a very amiable dragon, and nobody minded him. Had it come into the minds of

Rorie and Vixen to elope, Bates would not have barred their way. Indeed he would have been very glad to elope with them himself. The restricted license of the Abbey House had no charm for him.

Whither were those two drifting in the happy summer weather, lulled by the whisper of forest leaves faintly stirred by the soft south wind, or by the low murmur of the forest river, stealing on its stealthy course under overarching boughs, mysterious as that wondrous river in Kubla Khan's dream, and anon breaking suddenly out into a clamour loud enough to startle Arion as the waters came leaping and brawling over the shining moss-green boulders? Where were these happy comrades going as they rode side by side under the glancing lights and wavering shadows? Everybody knows what became of Launcelot and Guinevere after that famous ride of theirs. What of these two, who rode together day after day in sun and shower, who loitered and lingered in every loveliest nook in the Forest, who had the same tastes, the same ideas, the same loves, the same dislikes? Neither dared ask that question. They took the happiness fate gave them, and sought not to lift the veil of the future. Each was utterly and unreasonably happy, and each knew very well that this deep and entire happiness was to last no longer than the long summer days and the dangling balls of blossom on the beechen boughs. Before the new tufts on the fir-branches had lost their early green, this midsummer dream would be over. It was to be brief as a schoolboy's holiday.

What was the good of being so happy, only to be so much more miserable afterwards? A sensible young woman might have asked herself that question, but Violet Tempest did not. Her intentions were pure as the innocent light shining out of her hazel eyes—a gaze frank, direct, and fearless as a child's. She had no idea of tempting Roderick to be false to his vows. Had Lady Mabel, with her orchids and Greek plays, been alone in question, Violet might have thought of the matter more lightly: but filial duty was involved in Rorie's fidelity to his betrothed. He had promised his mother on her death-bed. That was a promise not to be broken.

One day—a day for ever to be remembered by Vixen and Rorie—a day that stood out in the foreground of memory's picture awfully distinct from the dreamy happiness that went before it, these two old friends prolonged their ride even later than usual. The weather was the loveliest that had ever blessed their journeyings—the sky Italian, the west wind just fresh enough to fan their cheeks, and faintly stir the green feathers of the ferns that grew breast-high on each side of the narrow track. The earth gave forth her subtlest perfumes under the fire of the midsummer sun. From Boldrewood the distant heights and valleys had an Alpine look in the clear bright air, the woods rising line above line in the far distance, in every shade of colour, from deepest umber to emerald green, from the darkest purple to translucent azure, yonder, where the farthest line of verdure met the sunlit sky. From Stony Cross the vast stretch of wood and moor lay basking in the warm vivid light, the yellow of the dwarf furze flashing in golden patches amidst the first bloom of the crimson heather. This southern corner of Hampshire was a glorious world to live in on such a day as this. Violet and her cavalier thought so, as their horses cantered up and down the smooth stretch of turf in front of The Forester's Inn.

"I don't know what has come to Arion," said Vixen, as she checked her eager horse in his endeavour to break into a mad gallop. "I think he must be what Scotch people call 'fey.'"

"And pray what may that mean?" asked Rorie, who was like the young lady made famous by Sydney Smith: what he did not know would have made a big book.

"Why, I believe it means that in certain moments of life, just before the coming of a great sorrow, people are wildly gay. Sometimes a man who is doomed to die breaks out into uproarious mirth, till his friends wonder at him. Haven't you noticed that sometimes in the accounts of suicides, the suicide's friends declare that he was in excellent spirits the night before he blew out his brains?"

"Then I hope I'm not 'fey,'" said Rorie, "for I feel uncommonly jolly."

"It's only the earth and sky that make us feel happy," sighed Violet, with a sudden touch of seriousness. "It is but an outside happiness after all."

"Perhaps not; but it's very good of its kind."

They went far afield that day; as far as the yews of Sloden; and the sun was low in the west when Vixen wished her knight good-bye, and walked her horse down the last long glade that led to the Abbey House. She was very serious now, and felt that she had transgressed a little by the length of her ride. Poor Bates had gone without his dinner, and that dismal yawn of his just now doubtless indicated a painful vacuity of the inner man. Rorie and she were able to live upon air and sunshine, the scent of the clover, and the freshness of the earth; but Bates was of the lower type of humanity, which requires to be sustained by beef and beer; and for Bates this day of sylvan bliss had been perhaps a period of deprivation and suffering.

Violet had been accustomed to be at home, and freshly dressed, in time for Mrs. Winstanley's afternoon tea. She had to listen to the accumulated gossip of the day—complaints about the servants, praises of Conrad, speculations upon impending changes of fashion, which threatened to convulse the world over which Theodore presided; for the world of fashion seems ever on the verge of a crisis awful as that which periodically disrupts the French Chamber.

To have been absent from afternoon tea was a breach of filial duty which the mild Pamela would assuredly resent. Violet felt herself doomed to one of those gentle lectures, which were worrying as the perpetual dropping of rain. She was very late—dreadfully late—the dressing-bell rang as she rode into the stable-yard. Not caring to show herself at the porch, lest her mother and the Captain should be sitting in the hall, ready to pronounce judgment upon her misconduct, she ran quickly up to her dressing-room, plunged her face into cold water, shook out her bright hair, brushed and plaited the long tresses with deft swift fingers, put on her pretty dinner-dress of pale blue muslin, fluttering all over with pale blue bows, and went smiling down to the drawing-room like a new Hebe, dressed in an azure cloud.

Mrs. Winstanley was sitting by an open window, while the Captain stood outside and talked to her in a low confidential voice. His face had a dark look which Vixen knew and hated, and his wife was listening with trouble in her air and countenance. Vixen, who meant to have marched straight up to her mother and made her apologies, drew back involuntarily at the sight of those two faces.

Just at this moment the dinner-bell rang. The Captain gave his wife his arm, and the two passed Vixen without a word. She followed them to the dining-room, wondering what was coming.

The dinner began in silence, and then Mrs. Winstanley began to falter forth small remarks, feeble as the twitterings of birds before the coming storm. How very warm it had been all day, almost oppressive: and yet it had been a remarkably fine day. There was a fair at Emery Down—at least not exactly a fair, but a barrow of nuts and some horrid pistols, and a swing. Violet answered, as in duty bound; but the Captain maintained his ominous silence. Not a word was said about Violet's long ride. It seemed hardly necessary to apologise for her absence, since her mother made no complaint. Yet she felt that there was a storm coming.

"Perhaps he is going to sell Arion," she thought, "and that's why the dear thing was 'fey.'"

And then that rebellious spirit of hers arose within her, ready for war.

"No, I would not endure that. I would not part with my father's last gift. I shall be rich seven years hence, if I live so long. I'll do what the young spendthrifts do. I'll go to the Jews. I will not be Captain Winstanley's helot. One slave is enough for him, I should think. He has enslaved poor mamma. Look at her now, poor soul; she sits in bodily fear of him, crumbling her bread

117

with her pretty fingers, shining and sparkling with rings. Poor mamma! it is a bad day for her when fine dresses and handsome jewels cannot make her happy."

It was a miserable dinner. Those three were not wont to be gay when they sat at meat together; but the dinner of to-day was of a gloomier pattern than usual. The strawberries and cherries were carried round solemnly, the Captain filled his glass with claret, Mrs. Winstanley dipped the ends of her fingers into the turquois-coloured glass, and disseminated a faint odour of roses.

"I think I'll go and sit in the garden, Conrad," she said, when she had dried those tapering fingers on her fringed doiley. "It's so warm in the house."

"Do, dear. I'll come and smoke my cigar on the lawn presently," answered the Captain.

"Can't you come at once, love?"

"I've a little bit of business to settle first. I won't be long!"

Mrs. Winstanley kissed her hand to her husband, and left the room, followed by Vixen.

"Violet," she said, when they were outside, "how could you stay out so long? Conrad is dreadfully angry."

"Your husband angry because I rode a few miles farther to-day than usual? Dear mother, that is too absurd. I was sorry not to be at home in time to give you your afternoon tea, and I apologise to you with all my heart; but what can it matter to Captain Winstanley?"

"My dearest Violet, when will you understand that Conrad stands in the place of your dear father?"

"Never, mamma, for that is not true. God gave me one father, and I loved and honoured him with all my heart. There is no sacrifice he could have asked of me that I would not have made; no command of his, however difficult, that I would not have obeyed. But I will obey no spurious father. I recognise no duty that I owe to Captain Winstanley."

"You are a very cruel girl," wailed Pamela, "and your obstinacy is making my life miserable."

"Dear mother, how do I interfere with your happiness? You live your life, and I mine. You and Captain Winstanley take your own way, I mine. Is it a crime to be out riding a little longer than usual, that you should look so pale and the Captain so black when I come home?"

"It is worse than a crime, Violet; it is an impropriety."

Vixen blushed crimson, and turned upon her mother with an expression that was half startled, half indignant.

"What do you mean, mamma?"

"Had you been riding about the Forest all those hours alone, it would have been eccentric—unladylike—masculine even. You know that your habit of passing half your existence on horseback has always been a grief to me. But you were not alone."

"No, mamma, I was not alone. I had my oldest friend with me; one of the few people in this big world who care for me."

"You were riding about with Roderick Vawdrey, Lady Mabel Ashbourne's future husband."

"Why do you remind me of his engagement, mamma? Do you think that Roderick and I have even forgotten it? Can he not be my friend as well as Lady Mabel's husband? Am I to forget that he and I played together as children, that we have always thought of each other and cared for each other as brother and sister, only because he is engaged to Lady Mabel Ashbourne?"

"Violet, you must know that all talk about brother and sister is sheer nonsense. Suppose I had set up brother and sister with Captain Winstanley! What would you—what would the world have thought?"

"That would have been different," said Vixen. "You did not know each other as babies. In fact you couldn't have done so, for you had left off being a baby before he was born," added Vixen naïvely.

"You will have to put a stop to these rides with Roderick. Everybody in the neighbourhood is talking about you."

"Which everybody?"

"Colonel Carteret to begin with."

"Colonel Carteret slanders everybody. It is his only intellectual resource. Dearest mother, be your own sweet easy-tempered self, not a speaking-tube for Captain Winstanley. Pray leave me my liberty. I am not particularly happy. You might at least let me be free."

Violet left her mother with these words. They had reached the lawn before the drawing-room windows. Mrs. Winstanley sank into a low basket-chair, like a hall-porter's, which a friend had sent her from the sands of Trouville; and Vixen ran off to the stables to see if Arion was in any way the worse for his long round.

The horses had been littered down for the night, and the stable-yard was empty. The faithful Bates, who was usually to be found at this hour smoking his evening pipe on a stone bench beside the stable pump, was nowhere in sight. Vixen went into Arion's loose-box, where that animal was nibbling clover lazily, standing knee-deep in freshly-spread straw, his fine legs carefully bandaged. He gave his mistress the usual grunt of friendly greeting, allowed her to feed him with the choicest bits of clover, and licked her hands in token of gratitude.

"I don't think you're any the worse for our canter over the grass, old pet," she cried cheerily, as she caressed his sleek head, "and Captain Winstanley's black looks can't hurt you."

As she left the stable she saw Bates, who was walking slowly across the court-yard, wiping his honest old eyes with the cuff of his drab coat, and hanging his grizzled head dejectedly.

Vixen ran to him with her cheeks aflame, divining mischief. The Captain had been wreaking his spite upon this lowly head.

"What's the matter, Bates?"

"I've lived in this house, Miss Voylet, man and boy, forty year come Michaelmas, and I've never wronged my master by so much as the worth of a handful o' wuts or a carriage candle. I was stable-boy in your grandfeyther's time, miss, as is well-beknown to you; and I remember your feyther when he was the finest and handsomest young squire within fifty mile. I've loved you and yours better than I ever loved my own flesh and blood: and to go and pluck me up by the roots and chuck me out amongst strangers in my old age, is crueller than it would be to tear up the old cedar on the lawn, which I've heard Joe the gardener say be as old as the days when such-like trees was fust beknown in England. It's crueller, Miss Voylet, for the cedar ain't got no feelings—but I feel it down to the deepest fibres in me. The lawn 'ud look ugly and empty without the cedar, and mayhap nobody'll miss me—but I've got the heart of a man, miss, and it bleeds."

Poor Bates relieved his wounded feelings with this burst of eloquence. He was a man who, although silent in his normal condition, had a great deal to say when he felt aggrieved. In his present state of mind his only solace was in many words.

"I don't know what you mean, Bates," cried Vixen, very pale now, divining the truth in part, if not wholly. "Don't cry, dear old fellow, it's too dreadful to see you. You don't mean—you can't mean—that—my mother has sent you away?"

"Not your ma, miss, bless her heart. She wouldn't sack the servant that saddled her husband's horse, fair weather and foul, for twenty years. No, Miss Voylet, it's Captain Winstanley that's given me the sack. He's master here, now, you know, miss."

"But for what reason? What have you done to offend him?"

"Ah, miss, there's the hardship of it! He's turned me off at a minute's notice, and without a character too. That's hard, ain't it, miss? Forty years in one service, and to leave without a character at last! That do cut a old feller to the quick."

"Why don't you tell me the reason, Bates? Captain Winstanley must have given you his reason for such a cruel act."

"He did, miss; but I ain't going to tell you."

"Why not, in goodness' name?"

"Because it's an insult to you, Miss Voylet; and I'm not going to insult my old master's granddaughter. If I didn't love you for your own sake—and I do dearly love you, miss, if you'll excuse the liberty—I'm bound to love you for the sake of your grandfeyther. He was my first master, and a kind one. He gave me my first pair o' tops. Lor, miss, I can call to mind the day as well as if it was yesterday. Didn't I fancy myself a buck in 'em."

Bates grinned and sparkled at the thought of those first top-boots. His poor old eyes, dim with years of long service, twinkled with the memory of those departed vanities.

"Bates," cried Vixen, looking at him resolutely, "I insist upon knowing what reason Captain Winstanley alleged for sending you away."

"He didn't allege nothing, miss: and I ain't agoing to tell you what he said."

"But you must. I order you to tell me. You are still my servant, remember. You have always been a faithful servant, and I am sure you won't disobey me at the last. I insist upon knowing what Captain Winstanley said; however insulting his words may have been to me, they will not surprise or wound me much. There is no love lost between him and me. I think everybody knows that. Don't be afraid of giving me pain, Bates. Nothing the Captain could say would do that. I despise him too much."

"I'm right down glad 'o that, miss. Go on a-despising of him. You can't give it him as thick as he deserves."

"Now, Bates, what did he say?"

"He said I was a old fool, miss, or a old rogue, he weren't quite clear in his mind which. I'd been actin' as go-between with you and Mr. Vawdrey, encouragin' of you to meet the young gentleman in your rides, and never givin' the Cap'en warnin', as your stepfeather, of what was goin' on behind his back. He said it was shameful, and you were makin' yourself the talk of the county, and I was no better than I should be for aidin' and abettin' of you in disgracin' yourself. And then I blazed up a bit, miss, and maybe I cheeked him: and then he turned upon me sharp and short and told me to get out of the house this night, bag and baggage, and never to apply to him for a character; and then he counted out my wages on the table, miss, up to this evening, exact to a halfpenny, by way of showing me that he meant business, perhaps. But I came away and left his brass upon the table, staring at him in the face. I ain't no pauper, praise be to God! I've had a good place and I've saved money: and I needn't lower myself by taking his dirty half-pence."

"And you're going away, Bates, to-night?" exclaimed Vixen, hardly able to realise this calamity.

That Captain Winstanley should have spoken insultingly of her and of Rorie touched her but lightly. She had spoken truly just now when she said that she scorned him too much to be easily wounded by his insolence. But that he should dismiss her father's old servant as he had sold her father's old horse; that this good old man, who had grown from boyhood to age under her ancestral roof, who remembered her father in the bloom and glory of early youth; that this faithful servant should be thrust out at the bidding of an interloper—a paltry schemer, who, in Vixen's estimation, had been actuated by the basest and most mercenary motives when he married her mother;—that these things should be, moved Violet Tempest with an overwhelming anger.

She kept her passion under, so far as to speak very calmly to Bates. Her face was white with suppressed rage, her great brown eyes shone with angry fire, her lips quivered as she spoke, and the rings on one clinched hand were ground into the flesh of the slender fingers.

"Never mind, Bates," she said very gently; "I'll get you a good place before ten o'clock to-night. Pack up your clothes, and be ready to go where I tell you two hours hence. But first saddle Arion."

"Bless yer heart, Miss Voylet, you're not going out riding this evening? Arion's done a long day's work."

"I know that; but he's fresh enough to do as much more—I've just been looking at him. Saddle him at once, and keep him ready in his stable till I come for him. Don't argue, Bates. If I knew that I were going to ride him to death I should ride him to-night all the same. You are dismissed without a character, are you?" cried Vixen, laughing bitterly. "Never mind, Bates, I'll give you a character; and I'll get you a place."

She ran lightly off and was gone, while Bates stood stock still wondering at her. There never was such a young lady. What was there in life that he would not have done for her were it to the shedding of blood? And to think he was no more to serve and follow her; no longer to jog contentedly through the pine-scented Forest—watching the meteoric course of that graceful figure in front of him, the lively young horse curbed by the light and dexterous hand, the ruddy brown hair glittering in the sunlight, the flexible form moving in unison with every motion of the horse that carried it! There could be no deeper image of desolation in Bates's mind than the idea that this rider and this horse were to be henceforth severed from his existence. What had he in life save the familiar things and faces among which he had grown from youth to age? Separate him from these beloved surroundings, and he had no standpoint in the universe. The reason of his being would be gone. Bates was as strictly local in his ideas as the zoophyte which has clung all its life to one rock.

He went to the harness-room for Miss Tempest's well-worn saddle, and brought Arion out of his snug box, and wisped him and combed him, and blacked his shoes, and made him altogether lovely—a process to which the intelligent animal was inclined to take objection, the hour being unseemly and unusual. Poor Bates sighed over his task, and brushed away more than one silent tear with the back of the dandy-brush. It was kind of Miss Violet to think about getting him a place; but he had no heart for going into a new service. He would rather have taken a room in one of the Beechdale cottages, and have dragged out the remnant of his days within sight of the chimney-stacks beneath which he had slept for forty years. He had money in the bank that would last until his lees of life were spilt, and then he would be buried in the churchyard he had crossed every Sunday of his life on his way to morning service. His kindred were all dead or distant—the nearest, a married niece, settled at Romsey, which good old humdrum market-town was—except once a week or so by carrier's cart—almost as unapproachable as the Bermudas. He was not going to migrate to Romsey for the sake of a married niece; when he could stop at Beechdale, and see the gables and chimneys of the home from which stern fate had banished him.

He had scarcely finished Arion's toilet when Miss Tempest opened the stable-door and looked in, ready to mount. She had her hunting-crop, with the strong horn hook for opening gates, her short habit, and looked altogether ready for business.

"Hadn't I better come with you, miss?" Bates asked, as he lifted her into her saddle.

"No, Bates. You are dismissed, you know. It wouldn't do for you to take one of Captain Winstanley's horses. He might have you sent to prison for horse-stealing."

"Lord, miss, so he might!" said Bates, grinning. "I reckon he's capable of it. But I cheeked him pretty strong, Miss Voylet. The thought o' that'll always be a comfort to me. You wouldn't ha' knowed me for your feyther's old sarvant if you'd heard me. I felt as if Satan had got hold o' my tongue, and was wagging it for me. The words came so pat. It seemed as if I'd got all the dictionary at the tip of my poor old tongue."

"Open the gate," said Vixen. "I am going out by the wilderness."

Bates opened the gate under the old brick archway, and Vixen rode slowly away, by unfrequented thickets of rhododendron and arbutus, holly and laurel, with a tall mountain-ash, or a stately deodora, rising up among them, here and there, dark against the opal evening sky.

It was a lovely evening. The crescent moon rode high above the tree-tops; the sunset was still red in the west. The secret depths of the wood gave forth their subtle perfume in the cool, calm air. The birds were singing in suppressed and secret tones among the low branches. Now and then a bat skimmed across the open glade, and melted into the woodland darkness, or a rabbit flitted past, gray and ghostlike. It was an hour when the woods assumed an awful beauty. Not to meet ghosts seemed stranger than to meet them. The shadows of the dead would have been in harmony with the mystic loveliness of this green solitude—a world remote from the track of men.

Even to-night, though her heart was swelling with indignant pain, Violet felt all the beauty of these familiar scenes. They were a part of her life, and so long as she lived she must love and rejoice in them. To-night as she rode quietly along, careful not to hurry Arion after his long day's work, she looked around her with eyes full of deep love and melancholy yearning. It seemed to her to-night that out of all that had been sweet and lovely in her life only these forest scenes remained. Humanity had not been kind to her. The dear father had been snatched away: just when she had grown to the height of his stout heart, and had fullest comprehension of his love, and greatest need of his protection. Her mother was a gentle, smiling puppet, to whom it were vain to appeal in her necessities. Her mother's husband was an implacable enemy. Rorie, the friend of her childhood—who might have been so much—had given himself to another. She was quite alone.

"The charcoal-burner in Mark Ash is not so solitary as I am," thought Vixen bitterly. "Charcoal-burning is only part of his life. He has his wife and children in his cottage at home."

By-and-by she came out of the winding forest ways into the straight high-road that led to Briarwood, and now she put her horse at a smart trot, for it was growing dark already, and she calculated that it must be nearly eleven o'clock before she could accomplish what she had to do and get back to the Abbey House. And at eleven doors were locked for the night, and Captain Winstanley made a circuit of inspection, as severely as the keeper of a prison. What would be said if she should not get home till after the gates were locked, and the keys delivered over to that stern janitor?

At last Briarwood came in sight above the dark clumps of beach and oak, a white portico, shining lamplit windows. The lodge-gate stood hospitably open, and Violet rode in without question, and up to the pillared porch.

Roderick Vawdrey was standing in the porch smoking. He threw away his cigar as Vixen rode up, and ran down the steps to receive her.

"Why, Violet, what has happened?" he asked, with an alarmed look.

It seemed to him, that only sudden death or dire calamity could bring her to him thus, in the late gloaming, pale, and deeply moved. Her lips trembled faintly as she looked at him, and for the moment she could find no words to tell her trouble.

"What is it, Violet?" he asked again, holding her gloved hand in his, and looking up at her, full of sympathy and concern.

"Not very much, perhaps, in your idea of things: but it seems a great deal to me. And it has put me into a tremendous passion. I have come to ask you to do me a favour."

"A thousand favours if you like; and when they are all granted, the obligation shall be still on my side. But come into the drawing-room and rest —and let me get you some tea—lemonade—wine—something to refresh you after your long ride."

"Nothing, thanks. I am not going to get off my horse. I must not lose a moment. Why it must be long after nine already, and Captain Winstanley locks up the house at eleven."

Rorie did not care to tell her that it was on the stroke of ten. He called in a stentorian voice for a servant, and told the man to get Blue Peter saddled that instant.

"Where's your groom, Violet?" he asked, wondering to see her unattended.

"I have no groom. That's just what I came to tell you. Captain Winstanley has dismissed Bates, at a minute's warning, without a character."

"Dismissed old Bates, your father's faithful servant! But in Heaven's name what for?"

"I would rather not tell you that. The alleged reason is an insult to me. I can tell you that it is not for dishonesty, or lying, or drunkenness, or insolence, or any act that a good servant need be ashamed of. The poor old man is cast off for a fault of mine; or for an act of mine, which Captain Winstanley pleases to condemn. He is thrust out of doors, homeless, without a character, after forty years of faithful service. He was with my grandfather, you know. Now, Rorie, I want you to take Bates into your service. He is not so ornamental as a young man, perhaps; but he is ever so much more useful. He is faithful and industrious, honest and true. He is a capital nurse for sick horses; and I have heard my dear father say that he knows more than the common run of veterinary surgeons. I don't think you would find him an incumbrance. Now, dear Rorie," she concluded coaxingly, with innocent childish entreaty, almost as if they had still been children and playfellows, "I want you to do this for me—I want you to take Bates."

"Why, you dear simple-minded baby, I would take a regiment of Bateses for your sake. Why this is not a favour——"

"'Tis as I should entreat you wear your gloves,'" cried Vixen, quoting Desdemona's speech to her general.

Rorie's ready promise had revived her spirit. She felt that, after all, there was such a thing as friendship in the world. Life was not altogether blank and dreary. She forgot that her old friend had given himself away to another woman. She had a knack of forgetting that little fact when she and Rorie were together. It was only in her hours of solitude that the circumstance presented itself distinctly to her mind.

"I am so grateful to you for this, Rorie," she cried. "I cannot tell you what a load you have taken off my mind. I felt sure you would do me this favour. And yet, if you had said No——! It would have been too dreadful to think of. Poor old Bates loafing about Beechdale, living upon his savings! I shall be able to pension him by-and-by, when I am of age; but now I have only a few pounds in the world, the remains of a quarter's pocket-money, according to the view and allowance of the forester," added Vixen, quoting the Forest law, with a little mocking laugh. "And now good-night; I must go home as fast as I can."

"So you must, but I am coming with you," answered Rorie; and then he roared again in his stentorian voice in the direction of the stables, "Where's that Blue Peter?"

"Indeed, there is no reason for you to come," cried Vixen. "I know every inch of the Forest."

"Very likely; but I am coming with you all the same."

A groom led out Blue Peter, a strong useful-looking hack, which Mr. Vawdrey kept to do his dirty work, hunting in bad weather, night-work, and extra journeys of all kinds. Rorie was in the saddle and by Vixen's side without a minute's lost time, and they were riding out of the grounds into the straight road.

They rode for a considerable time in silence. Vixen had seldom seen her old friend so thoughtful. The night deepened, the stars shone out of the clear heaven, at first one by one: and then, suddenly in a multitude that no tongue could number. The leaves whispered and rustled with faint mysterious noises, as Violet and her companion rode slowly down the long steep hill.

"What a beast that Winstanley is!" said Rorie, when they got to the bottom of the hill, as if he had been all this time arriving at an opinion about Violet's stepfather. "I'm afraid he must make your life miserable."

"He doesn't make it particularly happy," answered Vixen quietly; "but I never expected to be happy after mamma married. I did not think there was much happiness left for me after my father's death; but there was at least peace. Captain Winstanley has made an end of that."

"He is a wretch, and I should like to shoot him," said Rorie vindictively. "Dear little Vixen—yes, I must call you by the old pet name—to think that you should be miserable, you whom I remember so bright and happy, you who were born for happiness! But you are not always wretched, dear," he said, leaning over to speak to her in closer, more confidential tones, as if the sleepy birds and the whispering forest leaves could hear and betray him. "You were happy—we were happy—this morning."

He had laid his hand on hers. That useful Blue Peter needed no guidance. They were just leaving the road, and entering a long glade that led through a newly-opened fir plantation, a straight ride of a mile and a half or so. The young moon was gleaming cool and clear above the feathering points of the firs.

"Yes," she answered recklessly, involuntarily, with a stifled sob, "I am always happy with you. You are all that remains to me of my old life."

"My dearest, my loveliest, then be happy for ever!" he cried, winding his arm round her slim waist, and leaning over her till his head almost rested on her shoulder. Their horses were close together, walking at a foot-pace, Blue Peter in nowise disconcerted by this extraordinary behaviour of his rider.

"My love, if you can be happy at so small a price, be happy always!" said Rorie, his lips close to the girl's pale cheek, his arm feeling every beat of the passionate heart. "I will break the toils that bind me. I will be yours, and yours only. I have never truly loved anyone but you, and I have loved you all my life—I never knew how dearly till of late. No, dearest love, never did I know how utterly I loved you till these last summer days which we have lived together, alone and supremely happy, in the forest that is our native land. My Violet, I will break with Mabel to-morrow. She and I were never made for one other. You and I were. Yes, love, yes: we have grown up together side by side, like the primroses and violets in the woods. It is my second nature to love you. Why should we be parted? Why should I go on acting a dismal farce, pretending love to Mabel, pretending a friendship to you—alike false to both? There is no reason, Violet, none—except——"

"Except your promise to your dying mother," said Violet, escaping from his arm, and looking at him steadily, bravely, through the dim light. "You shall not break that for my sake—you ought not, were I ten times a better woman than I am. No, Rorie, you are to do your duty, and keep your word. You are to marry Lady Mabel, and be happy ever after, like the prince in a fairy tale. Depend upon it, happiness always comes in the long run to the man who does his duty."

"I don't believe it," cried Roderick passionately; "I have seen men who have done right ail through life—men who have sacrificed feeling to honour, and been miserable. Why should I imitate them? I love you. I loved you always; but my mother worried and teased me, vaunting Mabel's perfections, trying to lessen you in my esteem. And then, when she was dying, and it seemed a hard thing to oppose her wishes, or to refuse her anything, were it even the happiness of my life, I was weak, and let myself be persuaded, and sold myself into bondage. But it is not too late, Violet. I will write Mabel an honest letter to-morrow, and tell her the truth for the first time in my life."

"You will do nothing of the kind!" cried Violet resolutely. "What, do you think I have no pride—no sense of honour? Do you think I would let it be said of me, that I, knowing you to be engaged to your cousin, set myself to lure you away from her; that we rode together, and were seen together, happy in each other's company, and as careless of slander as if we had been brother and sister; and that the end of all was that you broke your faith to your promised wife in order to marry me? No, Rorie, that shall never be said. If I could stoop so low I should be worthy of the worst word my mother's husband could say of me."

"What does it matter what people say—your mother's husband above all? Malice can always find something evil to say of us, let us shape our lives how we may. What really matters is that we should be happy: and I can be happy with no one but you, Violet. I know that now. I will never marry Mabel

Ashbourne."

"And you will never marry me," answered Vixen, giving Arion a light touch of her whip which sent him flying along the shadowy ride.

Blue Peter followed as swiftly. Rorie was by Violet's side again in a minute, with his hand grasping hers.

"You mean that you don't love me?" he exclaimed angrily. "Why could you not have said so at the first; why have you let me live in a fool's paradise?"

"The paradise was of your own making," she answered. "I love you a little for the past, because my father loved you—because you are all that remains to me of my happy childhood. Yes, if it were not for you, I might look back and think those dear old days were only a dream. But I hear your voice, I look at you, and know that you are real, and that I once was very happy. Yes, Rorie, I do love you—love you—yes, with all my heart, dearer, better than I have ever loved anyone upon this earth, since my father was laid in the ground. Yes, dear." Their horses were walking slowly now; and her hand was locked in his as they rode side by side. "Yes, dear, I love you too well, and you and I must part. I had schooled myself to believe that I loved you only as I might have loved a brother; that you could be Lady Mabel's husband and my true friend. But that was a delusion—that can never be. You and I must part, Rorie. This night-ride in the Forest must be our last. Never any more, by sun or moon, must you and I ride together. It is all over, Rorie, the old childish friendship. I mean to do my duty, and you must do yours."

"I will never marry a woman I do not love."

"You will keep your promise to your mother; you will act as a man of honour should. Think, Rorie, what a shameful thing it would be to do, to break off an engagement which has been so long publicly known, to wound and grieve your good aunt and uncle."

"They have been very kind to me," sighed Rorie. "It would hurt me to give them pain."

His conscience told him she was right, but he was angry with her for being so much wiser than himself.

Then, in a moment, love—that had slumbered long, idly happy in the company of the beloved, and had suddenly awakened to know that this summer-day idlesse meant a passion stronger than death—love got the better of conscience, and he cried vehemently:

"What need I care for the Duke and Duchess! They can have their choice of husbands for their daughter; an heiress like Mabel has only to smile, and a man is at her feet. Why should I sacrifice myself, love, truth, all that makes life worth having? Do you think I would do it for the sake of Ashbourne, and the honour of being a duke's son-in-law?"

"No, Rorie, but for the sake of your promise. And now look, there is Lyndhurst steeple above the woods. I am near home, and we must say good-night."

"Not till you are at your own gate."

"No one must see you. I want to ride in quietly by the stables. Don't think I am ashamed of my errand to-night. I am not; but I want to save my mother trouble, and if Captain Winstanley and I were to discuss the matter there would be a disturbance."

Roderick Vawdrey seized Arion by the bridle.

"I shall not let you go so easily," he said resolutely. "Vixen, I have loved you ever since I can remember you. Will you be my wife?"

"No."

"Why did you say that you loved me?"

"Because I cannot tell a lie. Yes, I love you, Rorie; but I love your honour, and my own, better than the chance of a happiness that might fade and wither before we could grasp it. I know that your mother had a very poor opinion of me while she was alive; I should like her to know, if the dead know anything, that she was mistaken, and that I am not quite unworthy of her respect. You will marry Lady Mabel Ashbourne, Rorie: and ten years hence, when we are sober middle-aged people, we shall be firm friends once again, and you will thank and praise me for having counselled you to cleave to the right. Let go the bridle, Rorie, there's no time to lose. There's a glorious gallop from Queen's Bower to the Christchurch Road."

It was a long grassy ride, safe only for those who knew the country well, for it was bordered on each side by treacherous bogs. Violet knew every inch of the way. Arion scented his stable afar off, and went like the wind; Blue Peter stretched his muscular limbs in pursuit. It was a wild ride along the grassy track, beside watery marshes and reedy pools that gleamed in the dim light of a new moon. The distant woods showed black against the sky. There was no light to mark a human habitation within ken. There was nothing but night and loneliness and the solemn beauty of an unpeopled waste. A forest pony stood here and there—pastern-deep in the sedges—and gazed at those two wild riders, grave and gay, like a ghost. A silvery snake glided across the track; a water-rat plunged, with a heavy splash, into a black pool as the horses galloped by. It was a glorious ride. Miserable as both riders were, they could not but enjoy that wild rush through the sweet soft air, under the silent stars.

Vixen gave a long sigh presently, when they pulled up their horses on the hard road.

"I think I am 'fey' now," she said. "I wonder what is going to happen to me?"

"Whatever misfortunes come to you henceforth will be your own fault," protested Rorie savagely. "You won't be happy, or make me so."

"Don't be angry with me, Rorie," she answered quite meekly. "I would rather be miserable in my own way than happy in yours."

Arion, having galloped for his own pleasure, would now have liked to crawl. He was beginning to feel the effects of unusual toil, and hung his head despondently; but Vixen urged him into a sharp trot, feeling that matters were growing desperate.

Ten minutes later they were at the lodge leading to the stables. The gate was locked, the cottage wrapped in darkness.

"I must go in by the carriage-drive," said Vixen. "It's rather a bore, as I am pretty sure to meet Captain Winstanley. But it can't be helped."

"Let me go in with you."

"No, Rorie; that would do no good. If he insulted me before you, his insolence would pain me."

"And I believe I should pain him," said Rorie. "I should give him the sweetest horsewhipping he ever had in his life."

"That is to say you would bring disgrace upon me, and make my mother miserable. That's a man's idea of kindness. No, Rorie, we part here. Good-night, and—good-bye."

"Fiddlesticks!" cried Rorie. "I shall wait for you all to-morrow morning at the kennels."

Vixen had ridden past the open gate. The lodge-keeper stood at his door waiting for her. Roderick respected her wishes and stayed outside.

"Good-night," she cried again, looking back at him; "Bates shall come to you to-morrow morning."

The hall-door was wide open, and Captain Winstanley stood on the threshold, waiting for his stepdaughter. One of the underlings from the stable was ready to take her horse. She dismounted unaided, flung the reins to the groom, and walked up to the Captain with her firmest step. When she was in the hall he shut the door, and bolted and locked it with a somewhat ostentatious care. She seemed to breathe less freely when that great door had shut out the cool night. She felt as if she were in a jail.

"I should like half-a-dozen words with you in the drawing-room before you go upstairs," Captain Winstanley said stiffly.

"A hundred, if you choose," answered Vixen, with supreme coolness.

She was utterly fearless. What risks or hazards had life that she need dread? She hoped nothing—feared nothing. She had just made the greatest sacrifice that fate could require of her: she had rejected the man she fondly loved. What were the slings and arrows of her stepfather's petty malice compared with such a wrench as that?

She followed Captain Winstanley to the drawing-room. Here there was more air; one long window was open, and the lace curtains were faintly stirred by the night winds. A large moderator lamp burned upon Mrs. Winstanley's favourite table—her books and basket of crewels were there, but the lady of the house had retired.

"My mother has gone to bed, I suppose?" inquired Vixen.

"She has gone to her room, but I fear she is too much agitated to get any rest. I would not allow her to wait here any longer for you."

"Is it so very late?" asked Vixen, with the most innocent air.

Her heart was beating violently, and her temper was not at its best. She stood looking at the Captain, with a mischievous sparkle in her eyes, and her whip tightly clenched.

She was thinking of that speech of Rorie's about the "sweetest horsewhipping." She wondered whether Captain Winstanley had ever been horsewhipped; whether that kind of chastisement was numbered in the sum of his experiences. She opined not. The Captain was too astute a man to bring himself in the way of such punishment. He would do things that deserved horsewhipping, and get off scot free.

"It is a quarter-past eleven. I don't know whether you think that a respectable hour for a young lady's evening ride. May I ask the motive of this nocturnal expedition?"

"Certainly. You deprived Bates of a comfortable place—he has only been in the situation forty years—and I went to get him another. I am happy to say that I succeeded."

"And pray who is the chivalrous employer willing to receive my dismissed servant without a character?"

"A very old friend of my father's—Mr. Vawdrey."

"I thought as much," retorted the Captain. "And it is to Mr. Vawdrey you have been, late at night, unattended?"

"It is your fault that I went unattended. You have taken upon yourself to dismiss my groom—the man who broke my first pony, the man my father gave me for an attendant and protector, just as he gave me my horse. You will take upon yourself to sell my horse next, I suppose?"

"I shall take a great deal more upon myself, before you and I have done with each other, Miss Tempest," answered the Captain, pale with passion.

Never had Vixen seen him so strongly moved. The purple veins stood out darkly upon his pale forehead, his eyes had a haggard look; he was like a man consumed inwardly by some evil passion that was stronger than himself, like a man possessed by devils. Vixen looked at him with wonder. They stood facing each other, with the lamplit table between them, the light shining on both their faces.

"Why do you look at me with that provoking smile?" he asked. "Do you want to exasperate me? You must know that I hate you."

"I do," answered Vixen; "but God only knows why you should do so."

"Do you know no reason?"

"No."

"Can't you guess one?"

"No; unless it is because my father's fortune will belong to me by-and-by, if I live to be five-and-twenty, and your position here will be lessened."

"That is not the reason; no, I am not so base as that. That its not why I hate you, Violet. If you had been some dumpy, homely, country lass, with thick features and a clumsy figure, you and I might have got on decently enough. I would have made you obey me; but I would have been kind to you. But you are something very different. You are the girl I would have perilled my soul to win—the girl who rejected me with careless scorn. Have you forgotten that night in the Pavilion Garden at Brighton? I have not. I never look up at the stars without remembering it; and I can never forgive you while that memory lives in my mind. If you had been my wife, Violet, I would have been your slave. You forced me to make myself your stepfather; and I will be master instead of slave. I will make your life bitter to you if you thwart me. I will put a stop to your running after another woman's sweetheart. I will come between you and your lover, Roderick Vawdrey. Your secret meetings, your clandestine love-making, shall be stopped. Such conduct as you have been carrying on of late is a shame and disgrace to your sex."

"How dare you say that?" cried Vixen, beside herself with anger.

She grasped the lamp with both her hands, as if she would have hurled it at her foe. It was a large moon-shaped globe upon a bronze pedestal—a fearful thing to fling at one's adversary. A great wave of blood surged up into the girl's brain. What she was going to do she knew not; but her whole being was convulsed by the passion of that moment. The room reeled before her eyes, the heavy pedestal swayed in her hands, and then she saw the big moonlike globe roll on to the carpet, and after it, and darting beyond it, a stream of liquid fire that ran, and ran, quicker than thought, towards the open window.

Before she could speak or move, the flame had run up the lace curtain, like a living thing, swift as the flight of a bird or the gliding motion of a lizard. The wide casement was wreathed with light. They two—Vixen and her foe— seemed to be standing in an atmosphere of fire.

Captain Winstanley was confounded by the suddenness of the catastrophe. While he stood dumb, bewildered, Vixen sprang through the narrow space between the flaming curtains, as if she had plunged into a gulf of fire. He heard her strong clear voice calling to the stablemen and gardeners. It rang like a clarion in the still summer night.

There was not a moment lost. The stablemen rushed with pails of water, and directly after them the Scotch gardener with his garden-engine, which held several gallons. His hose did some damage to the drawing-room carpet and upholstery, but the strong jet of water speedily quenched the flames. In ten minutes the window stood blank, and black, and bare, with Vixen standing on the lawn outside, contemplating the damage she had done.

Mrs. Winstanley rushed in at the drawing-room door, ghostlike, in her white *peignoir*, pale and scared.

"Oh, Conrad, what has happened?" she cried distractedly, just able to distinguish her husband's figure standing in the midst of the disordered room.

"Your beautiful daughter has been trying to set the house on fire," he answered. "That is all."

CHAPTER XVI.

"That must end at once."

A quarter of an hour later, when all the confusion was over, Violet was kneeling by her mother's chair, trying to restore tranquillity to Mrs. Winstanley's fluttered spirits. Mother and daughter were alone together in the elder lady's dressing-room, the disconsolate Pamela sitting, like Niobe, amidst her scattered fineries, her pomade-pots and powder-boxes, fan-cases and jewel-caskets, and all the arsenal of waning beauty.

"Dear mother," pleaded Violet, with unusual gentleness, "pray don't give way to this unnecessary grief. You cannot surely believe that I tried to set this dear old home on fire—that I could be so foolish—granting even that I were wicked enough to do it—as to destroy a place I love—the house in which my father was born! You can't believe such a thing, mother."

"I know that you are making my life miserable," sobbed Mrs. Winstanley, feebly dabbing her forehead with a flimsy Valenciennes bordered handkerchief, steeped in eau-de-cologne, "and I am sure Conrad would not tell a falsehood."

"Perhaps not," said Vixen with a gloomy look. "We will take it for granted that he is perfection and could not do wrong. But in this case he is mistaken. I felt quite capable of killing him, but not of setting fire to this house."

"Oh," wailed Pamela distractedly, "this is too dreadful! To think that I should have a daughter who confesses herself at heart a murderess."

"Unhappily it is true, mother," said Vixen, moodily contrite. "For just that one moment of my life I felt a murderous impulse—and from the impulse to the execution is a very short step. I don't feel myself very superior to the people who are hanged at Newgate, I assure you."

"What is to become of me?" inquired Mrs. Winstanley in abject lamentation. "It is too hard that my own daughter should be a source of misery in my married life, that she should harden her heart against the best of stepfathers, and try, yes, actually try, to bring discord between me and the husband I love. I don't know what I have done that I should be so miserable."

"Dear mother, only be calm and listen to me," urged Violet, who was very calm herself, with a coldly resolute air which presently obtained ascendency over her agitated parent. "If I have been the source of misery, that misery cannot too soon come to an end. I have long felt that I have no place in this house—that I am one too many in our small family. I feel now—yes, mamma, I feel and know that the same roof cannot cover me and Captain Winstanley. He and I can no longer sit at the same board, or live in the same house. That must end at once."

"What complaint can you have to make against him, Violet?" cried her mother hysterically, and with a good deal more dabbing of the perfumed handkerchief upon her fevered brow. "I am sure no father could be kinder than Conrad would be to you if you would only let him. But you have set yourself against him from the very first. It seems as if you grudged me my happiness."

"It shall seem so no longer, mamma. I will cease to be a thorn in your garland of roses," replied Vixen, with exceeding bitterness. "I will leave the Abbey House directly any other home can be found for me. If dear old McCroke would take care of me I should like to go abroad, somewhere very far, to some strange place, where all things would be different and new to me," continued Vixen, unconsciously betraying that aching desire for forgetfulness natural to a wounded heart. "Sweden, or Norway, for instance. I think I should like to spend a year in one of those cold strange lands, with good old McCroke for my companion. There would be nothing to remind me of the Forest," she concluded with a stifled sob.

"My dear Violet, you have such wild ideas," exclaimed her mother with an injured air. "It is just as Conrad says. You have no notion of the proprieties. Sweden or Norway, indeed! Was there ever anything so outlandish? What would people say, I wonder?"

"Ah, what indeed, mamma. Perhaps, they might for once say what is true: that I could not get on with Captain Winstanley, and so was forced to find another home."

"And what a reproach that would be to me," cried her mother. "You are so selfish, Violet; you think of no one but yourself."

"Perhaps that is because nobody else thinks of me, mother."

"How can you say such abominable things, Violet? Am I not thinking of you this moment? I am sure I have thought of you this evening until my head aches. You force one to think about you, when you behave in such a disgraceful manner."

"What have I done that is disgraceful, mamma? I have ridden out at an unusual hour to get a place for an old servant—a man who has served in this house faithfully for forty years. That is what I have done, and I should not be ashamed if it were known to everybody in Hampshire. Yes, even to Lady Mabel Ashbourne, that pattern of chilly propriety. The disgrace is Captain Winstanley's. It is he who ought to be ashamed of turning off my father and grandfather's old servant. What you have to be sorry for, mamma, is that you have married a man capable of such an action."

"How dare you speak against him!" cried the offended wife. "He has done everything for the best. It was your own foolish conduct that obliged him to dismiss Bates. To think that a daughter of mine should have so little self-respect as to go roaming about the Forest with an engaged man! It is too dreadful."

"You need not make yourself unhappy about the engaged man, mamma," said Vixen scornfully. "He is out of danger. Rorie and I need never see each other again. I should be more than content that it should be so. Only arrange with Captain Winstanley for some allowance to be made me—just money enough to enable me to live abroad with dear old McCroke. I want no gaieties, I want no fine dresses, The simplest mode of life, in a strange country, will suit me best."

"I can't bear the idea of your going away," whimpered Mrs. Winstanley. "People will talk so. A stepfather's is such a delicate position. People are sure to say cruel things about Conrad. And it is all your fault, Violet. We might have lived so happily together if you had liked."

"We might, perhaps, mamma; but I don't think any of us knew the way. Captain Winstanley could hardly expect that to sell my father's favourite horse was the shortest way to my liking; and that's how he began his reign in this house. Don't let us talk any more, my dear mother. Words are useless to heal such wounds as ours. Good-night. Sleep well, and forget all about me. To-morrow you and the Captain can give me my liberty."

"I thought you were so fond of the Abbey House," moaned her mother.

"So I was when it was home. It has ceased to be my home, and I shall be glad to leave it."

"Oh, Violet, you have a hard heart."

"Good-night, mamma."

She was gone, leaving Mrs. Winstanley feebly moaning, and vaguely dabbing her forehead, feeling that the Fates had not been kind to her. Life seemed to have gone all askew. It was as if Theodore had taken to sending home misfits. Nothing was smooth or pleasant in an existence whose halcyon calm had once been undisturbed by so much as a crumpled rose-leaf.

Vixen went straight to her room, accompanied by Argus, who had followed her from the hall to the door of her mother's dressing-room, and had waited patiently for her in the corridor, with his head leaning against the closed door, as if he scented trouble within.

When girl and dog were alone together, Violet flung herself on the ground, threw her arms round the mastiff's thick neck, and let her tears flow freely against that faithful head.

"Oh, Argus," she cried piteously, "you are the only friend left me in this wide world!"

END OF VOL. II.